Murder in Cottage #6

A Liz Lucas Cozy Mystery - Book 1

BY

DIANNE HARMAN

Published by: Dianne Harman
www.dianneharman.com

Interior, cover design and website by
Vivek Rajan Vivek
www.vivekrajanvivek.com

ISBN: 978-1508924920

CONTENTS

ACKNOWLEDGMENTS

First of all, I want to thank you, my readers, who have made my books so popular. This is the first book in a new series, and I hope you'll enjoy this series as much as you've obviously enjoyed my other cozy mystery series, the Cedar Bay Cozy Mystery Series. There is nothing more gratifying for an author than to have readers tell them how much they enjoy their books or let the author know by buying other books in a series that they've enjoyed them. Your reviews are always appreciated. Thank you so much! I'd love to hear from you about this book or any of the others. Here's my email address: dianne@dianneharman.com.

I want to extend a special thanks to Vivek Rajan for the fabulous book covers he creates, his unending sound advice, and his taking the time to answer the multitude of questions I always have. I not only think of him as my editor, formatter, and marketing guru, I think of him as a friend and highly recommend him to other authors.

Finally, I want to thank my husband, Tom, for his support, belief in me, and love. He spends countless hours reading what I've written, and I value his thoughts and connemts. Without him, I wouldn't have the time and the freedom to spend doing what I love – writing! Thank you!

CHAPTER ONE

Sitting in her favorite chair in the great room of the lodge, Liz gazed out the large window that wrapped around the outside deck of the lodge. The view from the window was breathtaking, and she never tired of simply sitting and watching as the natural beauty of the scene before her constantly changed and unfolded. She heard the cries of sea gulls circling overhead, diving and twisting as they rode the air currents looking for a tasty morsel of food that might be floating on the ocean's surface.

The lodge and the adjacent spa were located about an hour north of San Francisco on the outskirts of the charming little town of Red Cedar. Perched nearly eighty feet above the ocean on a rocky point that jutted out into the ocean, it was a popular place for San Francisco residents to visit for some much-needed rest and relaxation. The great room where she was sitting contained a fully equipped kitchen at one end and a large wood-burning fireplace at the other end. One area of the great room contained comfortable upholstered chairs where guests could sit while enjoying the spectacular view and the surrounding scenery.

The section of the great room closest to the kitchen was furnished with a massive highly polished red cedar dining room table that had been hewn from a single slab of wood. The table easily accommodated twenty guests when the family style breakfast and evening meals were served.

Sipping her morning coffee, she heard the roar of the ocean as the waves crashed against the cliff far below. She turned her head slightly and had a clear view of several of the ten cottages which surrounded the lodge and spa and were set back among the towering red cedar trees. The beautiful ancient trees had been the reason she and Joe had named the spa the Red Cedar Spa when they bought it.

Joe had died almost a year earlier of a sudden heart attack, and now she was running the spa by herself with the help of her employees. Bertha was the manager, Zack was the handyman she relied on to keep things in working condition, and Sarah was the young woman who came daily to clean the cottages. Additionally, there were numerous employees that worked in the spa located just a few steps from the lodge. It was a lot of work, but she'd never regretted the day she and Joe decided to buy the spa. After he'd died, Jonah and Brittany, her two adult children, wanted her to sell it, telling her it was too much work for her to do alone.

She had loved the rustic spa and the surrounding cottages from the first moment she'd visited them when she and her friend of many years, Judy Rasmussen, had spent a long "girls' weekend" as guests at the spa. She smiled thinking back to what she'd thought when she first opened the door to their large cottage. *When the brochure said "cottage," I never expected something like this!*

Two king size beds were flanked by cedar chests used as nightstands. A large bathroom with a tiled shower was filled with numerous amenities from the spa. Each cottage had a view of the ocean on one side and the cedar forest on the other. Fluffy white towels and robes were neatly stacked on the marble counter for the guests to use.

She remembered overhearing the manager of the spa telling one of the employees that the then-owner of the spa was having financial problems and needed to sell the spa. When Liz returned to her home in the San Francisco area, she'd convinced Joe to sell his three auto dealerships in the city and start one in the small town of Red Cedar. The spa was located within the town boundaries, but the main business district was about a mile inland from the spa. It hadn't been very hard to convince him that the stress that came from owning the dealerships would be gone, and it would greatly benefit his health. She told him it would also make his doctor happy, because he was very concerned about Joe's health. His doctor had prescribed eight different types of pills for Joe's high blood pressure, "bad" cholesterol, and for his constant battle with stress management. But even with the medication and a strict low calorie diet, the condition of his health remained guarded.

Unfortunately, the move to a slower paced lifestyle in a rural area came too late for Joe. He'd been under extreme business pressure and stress for many years, and according to his cardiologist, his heart had suffered considerable damage. He died of a massive heart attack at his car agency in Red Cedar three years after they had moved to the area and purchased the spa.

Liz walked over to the kitchen counter and poured herself another cup of coffee as she reflected back on the events of the last year. Joe had used the services of a large law firm in San Francisco when they lived there. The attorney Joe worked with had handled the probate of his will, and one time when Liz was at the attorney's office she'd met a senior partner in the firm who specialized in criminal law cases. Roger was a widower, and one day he asked her to join him for a cup of coffee. They'd gotten along well, had gone out together on several casual dates, and he'd even come to the spa to visit her several times. She had mixed feelings about him. Part of her was very attracted to him, but when he indicated he'd like to take their relationship to a level that was beyond friendship, she struggled with feelings of being disloyal to the memory of her wonderful marriage to Joe. Even though it had been nearly a year since Joe died, she didn't know if she was ready to enter into the romantic type of relationship Roger was hinting at. They'd shared a few kisses, and she couldn't deny that there was a strong physical chemistry between them.

I know I'm going to have to make a decision fairly soon, and I think the answer is going to be yes, but I don't have to decide today. Anyway, Judy's coming up in a couple of days, and we're going to try some of the new treatments the spa has started offering. I'm ready for a little pampering.

Little did she know what the future held for her and what an important part Roger was going to play in her it.

CHAPTER TWO

Liz's reverie was broken by the sound of someone barging through the front door. She looked up and saw Bertha shaking and crying. "Bertha, what's wrong?" Bertha was crying so hard she wasn't able to answer.

Liz put her arm around her and led her to one of the chairs that surrounded the large cedar dining table. "What is it, Bertha? Has something bad happened?"

Bertha gulped and said, "I was in my office when I got a call from Delores at the spa. She said Mrs. Nelson hadn't checked in this morning for her 8:00 warm stone massage and asked if I would go over to cottage #6 and remind her of her appointment. I went over there and knocked on her cottage door several times. She never answered. You know I have the keys to all the cottages, and I keep them with me all the time, so I opened the door and saw her lying in bed. She wasn't moving. When I walked over to her I realized she wasn't breathing. She was dead."

Liz's hand flew up to her mouth. "Oh no! I can't believe it! Does anyone else know?"

"No. I came directly here from her cottage. She was in cottage number six. I locked the door when I left. I didn't know what else to do."

"That was exactly the right thing to do," Liz said, patting her hand. "Sit here for a minute and try to calm down. Did you notice anything out of place? Do you think she had a heart attack or something? I know the last few weeks have been very stressful for her what with Dave trying to win another term as mayor and the Red Cedar Tribune writing all those articles about him insinuating he was illegally skimming money from the city coffers. I didn't see her when she checked in yesterday, but she seemed perfectly normal last night when she was here with the other guests for dinner. She said she'd loved her facial and massage treatments and was looking forward to having two more today and then going home after she had her last treatment this afternoon."

"Liz, there was a half-empty bottle of Jack Daniels on the nightstand next to her bed. Do you think maybe she mixed sleeping pills and alcohol and committed suicide? I just don't know what to think," Bertha said, her brown eyes large with fright against her pale complexion.

"Let me get you a cup of coffee. I really need to call Seth Williams and report this."

I don't want to have anything to do with that lecherous obese stupid man, but I don't have a choice. He is the chief of police and having the mayor's wife found dead in one of my cottages is something he needs to know about immediately.

*****

"Red Cedar Police Department. How may I direct your call?" the young receptionist asked.

"I'd like to speak with Chief Williams. Please tell him Liz Lucas is calling," she said, nervously twisting a strand of her auburn hair.

The receptionist put her on hold, and a few moments later she heard Seth's oily voice. "Liz, to what do I owe the pleasure of your call? I'm hopin' you're gonna tell me yer finally goin' to accept the long-standin' dinner invitation I've been offerin' for the last few months."

When pigs fly, Liz thought. *I need him to be on my side right now, so I better make nice. If word gets out that someone died here at the spa, it sure could be bad for business. I need to think about damage control, and Seth can provide that if I sweet talk him.*

"I wish it was something enjoyable like that," she said in a sultry honey-toned voice, "but actually Seth, I have a little problem out here at the spa and need you to come out here right away."

"If it involves you, I'll be there soon as I can. Wanna give me a head's up what this is all about, pretty lady?"

"No. It can wait until you get here. Can you come in your personal car, not your patrol car? I really don't want the guests to see a police car on the premises. It might upset them."

"Sure can. Sounds interestin'. Keep in mind I'm real partial to black lace. See you in a few."

Yuck. I can't stand that smarmy man, and now I'm going to have to deal with him.

She ended the call and turned to where Bertha was standing. "Bertha, you heard my conversation. Seth will be here in a few minutes. Why don't you tell Sarah you'll make the box lunches for the guests who can't get into town for lunch because they've booked back-to-back treatments? That might help to take your mind off of what you just saw. I imagine Seth will want to take a statement from you, and I probably better go into town and tell the mayor that his wife is dead. Not something I really want to do. Go on into the kitchen and I'll let you know when Seth gets here."

She walked down the stairs to the lower level of the lodge where her personal living quarters were located. *I need to get out of these pajamas and robe. Black lace? I don't think so. Jeans and a sweater will work just fine. That man has a sick mind. Between the mayor and Seth, I am definitely not looking forward to the next few hours. And how am I going to keep the guests from finding out?*

CHAPTER THREE

Fifteen minutes later Seth came swaggering through the front door of the lodge, his thumbs hooked just inside his dark blue uniform pants that hung below a large belly which was threatening to pop the lower buttons of his blue uniform shirt. Gray, oily hair hung in tufts below a battered black police chief hat with a silver emblem inscribed "Red Cedar Police Chief."

Liz couldn't help but notice the big yellow stain on his shirt. "See yer lookin' at that spot on my shirt," Seth said. "Egg yolk slipped off my fork this mornin' when I was havin' my usual breakfast of ham and eggs at Gertie's Diner. Jes' one of those things that seems to happen all the time to me. Ya' know what I mean?"

"Seth, thank you so much for coming out here on such short notice. I have a little problem, and I'm not real sure what to do about it. Please, follow me."

"Ain't seein' any black lace on ya'. I'll git ya' some if ya' like. I read the Victoria's Secret catalogue from cover to cover every month. You'd look good in some of them things they got for sale."

Ignoring Seth's uncouth remarks, Liz walked out the door and almost tripped over what she privately called the "spa dog," even though his name was Brandy Boy. A massive St. Bernard, weighing over one hundred sixty pounds, he was a favorite of the guests who

8

visited the spa.

Although the original St. Bernard dogs were bred by Augustine monks as rescue dogs in the snowy and cold Swiss Alps, Brandy Boy had little interest in any type of task that involved physical activity. The previous owner who sold the spa to Joe and Liz had asked them to keep Brandy Body because he couldn't take the big dog with him. Despite his seemingly constant slobbering and drooling, Liz had grown attached to the big loveable brown and white giant who spent most of his time sleeping on the porch. He rarely acknowledged anyone going in or out the door other than to open his eyes when it slammed.

Occasionally a guest wanted to take a hike on one of the many trails that led into the forest from the lodge. Liz always recommended that he or she take Brandy Boy along to act as an informal guide. Even though he was the easiest going dog in the world, he knew which trails were safe to travel and which ones weren't. Many a guest had returned to the spa from their hike marveling that Brandy Boy had physically led the way and showed the guest which trail was the right one to take to return to the lodge.

Just like the famous rescue dogs in the Swiss Alps, the prior owner had equipped Brandy Body with a dog collar that had a small wooden cask attached to it. If a guest was in a cottage and wanted an after dinner brandy, he or she could call the lodge, and Brandy Boy would be dispatched to the cottage with the "rescue" brandy. When given the proper command, he even knew which cottage needed the delivery. Each cottage had a supply of dog treats that were to be given to Brandy Boy as a reward after he made his delivery.

When they first bought the spa, Joe thought Brandy Boy was too big to sleep indoors, and he'd asked Zack, the handyman, to build a dog house for him. The huge dog house was located next to the lodge and at any given time you could find Brandy Boy either sleeping in his dog house or lolling around on the front porch of the lodge. Having the dog house near the lodge was an arrangement which worked out well for everyone. With his ancestors having come from the Swiss Alps, Brandy Boy was happy and content to stay outside in his dog house year round, regardless of any inclement weather conditions.

After nearly tripping over Brandy Boy, Liz and Seth walked past the large rustic spa building with flowers spilling out of containers on either side of the front door and down the steps. Each of the ten cottages located on the premises was a smaller version of the spa, constructed as log cabin type structures with bright colored flowers surrounding them. Liz wanted the spa and cottages to project a warm welcoming feeling for the spa guests when they came for their stay, each of them hoping to leave refreshed and rejuvenated.

She stopped at a cottage with a brass #6 on the front door. "Seth, Dave Nelson's wife, Barbara, is in here. Dave told her she'd worked so hard on his campaign he was giving her a two day stay at the spa as a thank you gift. He wanted her to come here, have some treatments, and relax. My manager found her this morning. She's dead."

"What the...?"

"I know, Bertha and I are as shocked as you are. I don't know what happened."

"Sheesh. I was jes' with Dave and Barbara night before last at his victory party down at the Elks Lodge. Barbara seemed fine then. She was probably jes' glad his girlfriend didn't show up at the celebration. When did Barbara get here?"

"She checked in yesterday morning, had two spa treatments, and ate dinner at the lodge with the other guests last night." Liz put her key in the lock and opened the door. They both stared at Barbara lying in the bed. Liz noticed the half-empty bottle of Jack Daniels on the nightstand that Bertha had told her about.

Seth walked over to Barbara. "Yup, she's deader 'n a doornail. Better call the coroner. Ain't nothin' no one can do fer her now."

"Wait a minute. What kind of a vehicle will he come in? I really would like to avoid having to tell the other guests about this until we know more."

"He drives a big white van. Looks kinda like a bread delivery truck. Guess it kinda is, if ya' know what I mean. Ain't much difference between deliverin' a loaf of bread and deliverin' dead bodies," he said laughing obscenely. "Yer' guests'll just think someone's deliverin' somethin' to you."

Liz steeled herself not to comment on his insensitivity. *This man is disgusting,* she thought. *Is he the best the city of Red Cedar can do? And what was that reference to Dave's girlfriend all about?*

"Go ahead and call him. How long do you think it will be before he can come out here?"

"Don't know. I'll call him now, and then I need to call Leroy, my deputy chief. Need to figure out what in the blazes happened out here, although it looks pretty obvious to me." He punched in a number on his cell phone and she heard him say, "Wes, got a cold one out here at the Red Cedar Spa. Dave's wife. How soon can ya' be here?" He hung up and turned to Liz. "He'll be here in about fifteen minutes. Give me a minute while I call Leroy, then I'll need to ask ya' some questions."

He spoke with Leroy who carried the ceremonial title of deputy chief, which had been bestowed on him by Seth in exchange for passing on a pay raise, but he was actually nothing more than a patrol deputy on the small six man Red Cedar police force. After talking to Leroy for a few minutes he turned to her. "Sorry, Liz, but he's gonna have to drive a police car over here cuz his personal car broke down this mornin' while he was drivin' to work. No big surprise there. Dang thing's been smokin' like a chimney for the last two weeks."

"Well, I guess that can't be helped. Hopefully, the guests will be in town or having a spa treatment."

Seth took a stubby pencil and a tattered notebook out of his shirt pocket. He flipped the notebook open to an empty page that appeared to have a catsup stain on it and asked Liz, "Who discovered the body?"

"My manager, Bertha."

"Wouldja call her and tell her to get over here? Gonna need to get a statement from her. Ya' said Barbara had two spa treatments yesterday. Need to talk to the people who gave her them treatments."

Liz called Delores, the spa receptionist. "This is Mrs. Lucas. Would you check the reservation book and tell me what treatments Barbara Nelson had yesterday?"

She listened for a moment. "Are Gina and Cindy free, or are they busy with clients?" She waited while Delores checked the reservation book. "Good. Please ask both of them to come to cottage #6 immediately. I also want you to have them bring the spa registration form that Barbara Nelson filled out yesterday. Thanks."

A few minutes later Bertha came to the cottage, still clearly shaken by the morning's events. She was followed by Gina and Cindy who handed Liz the spa registration form for Barbara Nelson.

"Good morning, Seth," Bertha said.

"Hey, Bertha. Liz tells me you was the one who found Barbara. Need ya' to tell me everything." Bertha related to Seth essentially what she'd told Liz earlier.

When it was obvious that Seth wasn't going to ask Bertha any more questions, Liz said, "Bertha, you can go now. I think he's through with you. I'll stay here while he talks to Gina and Cindy and I also want to be here to find out what the coroner has to say about the cause of death."

"Ladies," Seth said to Gina and Cindy, "wanna know what kind of treatments Barbara had and if she seemed to be okay when you saw her yesterday."

"I saw her yesterday morning at 10:00," Cindy said. "She'd requested the stress-releasing massage. She was fine while she was with me and was feeling good when she left. She didn't say or do anything that seemed unusual to me. There's really nothing more I can tell you," Cindy said

Seth turned to Gina. "How about you?"

"Pretty much like Cindy just said. I saw her at 3:00 yesterday afternoon. She had a facial and purchased some beauty products from the spa that I recommended. She was quiet during the facial, thanked me when I was finished, and left. Other than that, I don't know anything about her."

"Thank you ladies. You can go back to the spa now. If I got any more questions, I'll get back to ya', but I'm pretty sure I know what happened to her."

He had just finished getting statements from Cindy and Gina when a white van drove up the narrow lane that led to the lodge and spa followed by a Red Cedar police car. They pulled to a stop next to cottage #6.

"Hey," Seth said as they got out of their respective vehicles, "Wes, Leroy. Stiff's in there. Got a statement from Liz and Bertha as well as the two wimmin who treated her at the spa yesterday. Leroy, you go in, and see what you can find. Probably better wear gloves, but there's not much to dust. Maybe ya' oughta do that Jack Daniels bottle in there. When you finish with it, take it back to the station. We oughta send a sample of the contents to the state police lab for testin', but I reckon me and you might have to do a little testin' of that Jack Daniels ourselves. Hate to let good booze go to waste, if ya' know what I mean. Wes, like to know what ya' think caused her death, but it seems purty black and white to me. Be willin' to bet she decided to buy the farm when she found out Dave had the hots for Darcy. Whole town knows they've been gettin' it on. Maybe she jes' found out. Decided to come out here and mix a little Black Jack with a handful of night-night pills and bingo, the deed is done."

Who is this Darcy woman? Liz thought. *I wonder if Barbara knew about the affair? And if she was going to commit suicide, why would she buy beauty products from the spa? Could Seth be right, that she came here to end her life? If that's true, sure wish she'd gone to another spa. I don't need this kind of publicity.*

Liz took a couple of deep breaths and a few minutes later followed the men into the cottage. She walked over to the coroner and asked, "Wes, do you have any idea what caused her death?"

"No. There's no sign of a struggle or foul play of any kind. Leroy quickly examined the door, and he said he didn't see any signs of forcible entry or that the lock had been tampered with. I'll know more after I do an autopsy on her. Maybe it's like Seth thinks, that she took some sleeping pills and combined it with the alcohol, although I don't see any prescription bottles. I understand she ate dinner at your lodge last night. Did you serve anything that might have caused her to suffer an allergic reaction? Sometimes a severe allergic reaction can lead to anaphylactic shock and death."

"I don't think so. I served the guests wine with several different kinds of cheeses and crackers. Dinner consisted of lamb chops baked in a wine sauce, broccoli with almonds, a rice pilaf, and an ice cream sundae with caramel sauce. When guests come to the spa they have to fill out a registration form and one of the things they're asked is if they have any food allergies. I know people can have life threatening allergies to things like peanuts or shellfish, so I'm very careful to always check each guest's registration form and make a note if they have any food allergies. Barbara wrote on her registration form that she wasn't allergic to anything. The people who work in the spa also have each guest fill out a general health form, and one of the questions asked is if they're allergic to any beauty products or chemical substances. According to what she filled out on her form, she wasn't allergic to anything."

"Well, we probably won't know anything until I complete the autopsy tomorrow. I have another one I need to do today. Dave been told yet?"

"No. I wanted to wait until I talked to you. I'm planning on going to his insurance agency and telling him shortly."

"Liz, be happy to do it for ya', course you'd owe me somethin' in return, if you know what I mean," Seth said suggestively.

"No. Since it happened on my property, I should be the one to tell him."

Wes took a gurney out of the back of the van and rolled it into the cottage. He and Leroy carefully transferred Barbara from the bed to the gurney and then pushed the gurney out to the van and loaded her body into it through the open rear doors. When they were finished, Wes drove back down the lane to the highway leading to town with Leroy following.

"I'll be goin' now, Liz," Seth said. "Ain't no more I can do 'til I get the results of the autopsy from Wes. Nice seein' ya', and don't forget about that invitation to dinner or my offer to get ya' a little somethin' from Victoria's Secret."

"Believe me, Seth, I won't forget. Thanks for getting out here so fast."

Liz looked around as he drove down the lane, thankful that it looked like no one had seen the police car or the unusual activity going on at cottage #6.

When she returned to the lodge, she called Bertha. "Would you please tell Sarah to clean up cottage #6?"

CHAPTER FOUR

Red Cedar was a small town and even though Liz had never been to Dave Nelson's office, she knew that the office in the early 20th century building with the red awning and the words "Dave Nelson Insurance Agency" was his. On her way she passed Gertie's Diner, known as the "in" place to find out the latest rumors about anything happening in the small town. People from as far away as San Francisco were known to come to Gertie's for the rich chocolate malted milk shakes and thick juicy burgers.

She smiled as she drove by the other shops that were owned by some of the more interesting and colorful townspeople of Red Cedar. There was the Custom Candle Shop, run by Nate, who had retired from his job working on the docks of San Francisco. Everyone who entered the shop was startled to see that it was owned by one of the biggest and hairiest men around with a smile that could light up a city block.

Then there was Walt's Western Shop, a wannabe cowboy shop owned by Walt, a former Chicago stock broker, who at age sixty decided to do what he'd always wanted to do – play like he was a cowboy. The shop was stocked with anything and everything a customer who had dreams of becoming a cowboy could want – from spurs to Stetson hats.

When she passed Susie's Hair Salon, she made a mental note to make an appointment to get her hair colored. At age fifty-two Liz was still a very attractive woman, short and full-figured, but her auburn hair had always been her best feature, even if she did need a little help from Susie to keep its deep rich color. Thick and lustrous, it framed her alabaster complexion and accentuated her sea green eyes and dark double fringed eyelashes.

As she pulled into the diagonal parking space a few shops down from the Dave Nelson Insurance Agency, she noticed the sign for Red Cedar Antiques and Art and remembered that Barbara Nelson and her partner owned the shop.

When I finish with Dave, I need to go in there. I should tell her partner about Barbara before she finds out from someone else.

She took a deep breath and opened the door of her van. When she walked into the insurance agency, she was greeted by an older rail-thin stony-faced woman with pink rimmed eyeglasses on a chain perched on the end of her long nose. "May I help you?" the woman asked. The nameplate on her desk read, "Rosie."

"My name is Liz Lucas. I'd like to see Dave Nelson. I don't have an appointment. This is a personal matter."

The woman looked Liz up and down. "Want to tell me what's so personal? I'm his secretary. Been with him for twenty years. He's not here, anyway. Took an early lunch like he does most days," she harrumphed.

"I'm afraid I have some bad news. His wife was found dead this morning. I'm the owner of the Red Cedar Spa, and Mrs. Nelson was a guest at the spa. Her body was discovered earlier this morning by one of my employees."

Rosie half stood up and then sat back down, obviously struggling to keep her composure. "I told him if he kept seeing…"

"I'm sorry I didn't understand you," Liz said.

"It was nothing. I didn't mean to say anything. It doesn't matter now, anyway."

"Could you tell me where I could find Mr. Nelson? I really don't want him to find out about this from someone passing on a rumor made up of half-truths."

"Usually goes home at lunchtime. I'd knock real loud if I were you. May take him a little while to answer the door," she said cryptically.

"I'm not sure I know where he lives. Would you mind giving me his address?"

"He lives two streets over. 417 Cedar Road. You can't miss his house. It's the big white one in the middle of the block with a grey roof. His silver colored Ford pickup truck will probably be in the driveway along with another car."

"Thank you," Liz said as she left.

That was weird. I think she said, "I told him if he kept seeing." Wonder what that was all about.

A few minutes later she parked her minivan on the street in front of Dave Nelson's house. In addition to the Ford pickup truck, there was a red convertible in the driveway. She walked up the steps and rang the doorbell. When there was no response, Liz knocked as loud as she could, certain that someone must be in the house if there were two cars in the driveway. Finally she heard footsteps coming towards the door and a male voice asked, "Who is it?"

"It's Liz Lucas. I'm the owner of the Red Cedar Spa, and I need to speak to Dave Nelson about his wife."

"Just a moment," the voice said. She stood waiting for several long minutes and then the front door was finally opened by the man she recognized as Dave Nelson from his campaign photos.

"May I come in?" she asked.

"Yes, of course. I'm sorry. I don't know where my manners are. What can I do for you, Mrs. Lucas?"

"Mr. Nelson, I'm sorry to have to be the one to tell you this, but Mrs. Nelson was found dead this morning at the Red Cedar Spa. She was discovered by my manager when she didn't check in for her spa reservation."

He blinked several times and then staggered backwards, landing on a nearby couch. "Barbara dead? Are you sure it was her?"

"Yes. She had dinner with the other guests and me at the lodge last night. She told us how happy she was with the spa gift you'd given her as a thank you for helping you win the election. After dinner was finished she retired to the cottage where she was staying. That's where she was found."

"I can't believe this. She was fine when she left yesterday morning. Do you know what she died from?"

"No. The police chief and the coroner were out at the spa this morning. The coroner is going to do an autopsy tomorrow. I imagine we'll know more then."

"Dave, what's going on?" asked a female voice which came from an adjoining room.

Liz heard high heels clicking on the wooden hallway floor and turned her head just as a beautiful brunette woman walked into the living room.

"I heard voices and wondered who was here." She walked over to Liz and extended her hand. "Hi! I'm Darcy Martinez, the principal of Red Cedar High School. Dave has been helping me over at the high school by talking to some of our seniors about different occupations and careers they can pursue when they graduate. And you are?"

"I'm Liz Lucas, the owner of the Red Cedar Spa."

"Nice to meet you. I've been meaning to get out there one of these days and treat myself to a little rest and relaxation." She looked at her watch. "Dave, I have to get back to school. Lunch break time is almost over. Is something wrong? You don't look very good."

"Darcy, Barbara was found dead this morning at the Red Cedar Spa. They don't know what she died from."

"Oh, honey, that's terrible news. I'm so sorry. I hate to leave you at a moment like this, but I really do have to get back to the high school. Nice to meet you, Mrs. Lucas. Come by the high school some time. Maybe you could talk to some of the seniors," she said as she walked out the front door.

Honey? That's weird. Dave doesn't even seem aware she said it. His grief seems genuine.

"Mr. Nelson, can I call someone for you? Or take you somewhere?"

"Yes. Here's my sister's phone number. If you could call her, I'd appreciate it."

Liz punched the numbers into her cell phone and told his sister what had happened. "Mr. Nelson, she'll be here in a few minutes. Is there anything else I can do for you?"

"No. Thank you for taking the time to come to my home and tell me in person. I'll be fine. It's just such a shock."

"Stay where you are. I'll let myself out. Again, I'm sorry."

CHAPTER FIVE

Liz got out of her car and looked at the front of the Red Cedar Antiques and Art shop, surprised at not only how large it was, but at the caliber of the merchandise. The front window had a display of brightly colored pottery, Arts and Craft style furniture, stained glass lamps that looked to Liz's untrained eye like real Tiffany lamps, and other decorative pieces, all beautifully arranged in a room setting.

"Hi, may I help you with something?" the attractive blond woman asked Liz when she walked into the store.

"I had no idea your shop had antiques of this quality. When I used to live in San Francisco, I loved to go to some of the antique shops and just look around. I fell in love with the Arts and Crafts style furniture and accessories. You have an incredible collection of them. Red Cedar is such a small town I'm amazed your shop can carry this caliber of merchandise. Do you have a lot of customers from the San Francisco area?"

"Yes. We have quite a number of San Francisco clients. What most people don't realize is there are a lot of ranches and old homes in this area that were built about the time the Arts and Crafts movement became popular in the early 20th century. That was the style of furniture and accessories the residents bought in those days. Many of the younger people who inherited the houses and the furniture want newer furnishings and we've developed a reputation for buying Arts and Crafts style furniture and accessories at fair prices. It works both ways. The sellers know we're fair and the buyers know we have good quality merchandise. I guess you could say it's a win-win for everyone."

"From what you're saying, am I to understand that you're one of the owners?"

"Yes. My name is Linda Wright. I'm the co-owner of the shop along with my partner, Barbara Nelson."

"I'm Liz Lucas, the owner of the Red Cedar Spa. I'm afraid I have some bad news. Barbara Nelson's body was discovered by my manager this morning in one of the cottages at the spa where she was staying. She was dead."

Linda's face visibly paled and she sat down heavily in a nearby chair. "I can't believe it. I just saw her night before last at Dave's victory party, and she was fine. Do you have any idea what caused her death? To my knowledge she was in excellent health."

"No. The coroner found no marks on her body that would indicate any foul play. The lock on the door didn't appear to have been tampered with. The police chief thinks maybe it was suicide. There was a bottle of Jack Daniels on the nightstand next to her bed."

"No, that just can't be. Barbara hated hard liquor. The only thing she ever drank was wine and maybe on a special occasion, a glass of champagne. It is absolutely not possible that she would have taken her own life by drinking excessively. Is the coroner going to do an autopsy on her body?"

"Yes. He said he couldn't get to it today, but he's scheduled it for tomorrow. Why do you ask?"

"I can't help but think she was murdered. Barbara was in perfect health and a very strong Catholic. She would never commit suicide. I have no idea why, but I think someone put the bottle there to make it look like it was suicide, but I'd bet every penny I have it wasn't."

"Have you noticed anything strange about her in the last few days? Was she having problems? Did she share anything with you?"

Linda looked down and suddenly seemed to develop an interest in her fingers, while avoiding eye contact with Liz. "What do you mean?" she asked.

"Well, I've heard rumors that Dave was having an affair. That may be all it is, a rumor. I'm wondering if Barbara had heard the same."

"Nothing new there. Barbara had heard the rumors for a long time. This time it…"

"You just said, 'this time it.' Are you implying that there had been other affairs before this one?"

"Barbara learned long ago she would never be the only woman in Dave's life. As I mentioned, she's a very strong Catholic and she simply decided she would stay with him no matter what. She was sure he would never divorce her for his current 'flavor of the month' as Barbara called them. He always came back, repentant, and promising never to do it again. I think she really believed him when he made those kinds of promises to her. Plus, she liked being the mayor's wife. In a town as small as Red Cedar that's a pretty big deal."

"I can see how it would be. I know you haven't had time to think about it, but will Barbara's death have some adverse effect on your business? Can you run it by yourself without Barbara as your partner?"

"Yes. The business is in my name. Barbara was a partner in name only, but because she was from a family whose roots go back to the founding fathers of this town, it was advantageous for me to bring her in as a partner. She knew everyone for miles around, plus she had great instincts and was very knowledgeable about the Arts and Crafts movement. I only know of one time when her knowledge was questioned." She paused. "Never mind, forget I said that." Whatever she was finding of interest in her fingers intensified.

"Linda, I'm not trained in law enforcement, but from what you're telling me you seem certain that Barbara didn't commit suicide. For all we know, she may have died of natural causes, but you also told me she was in excellent health. If she didn't commit suicide, and she was in excellent health and now she's dead, that leaves one conclusion, that someone may have murdered her. If that's true, the reputation of my spa is at stake. Please tell me what you know."

"I can't see where this would have anything to do with her death, but a few weeks ago she bought a Tiffany style lamp from a man who inherited a ranch from his grandfather. It was in the ranch house. He needed money to maintain the ranch and sold us the lamp. His grandfather had told him several times that the lamp was an original Tiffany lamp. It was beautiful. Barbara was pretty knowledgeable about Tiffany lamps, and she agreed with the young man's grandfather, that it was an original and the work on it was extraordinary. She bought it for $20,000 and called one of our clients in San Francisco who collected Tiffany items. He came up the shop and bought the lamp for $48,000. Naturally, we were thrilled. Matter of fact, I think that was one of those times we shared a glass of champagne to celebrate the sale, as it was one of our largest. Last week the buyer called and said he had the lamp appraised, and the appraiser told him it was not an authentic Tiffany lamp. Barbara told him the appraiser was wrong. He asked for his money back, and she refused because she was certain the lamp was authentic. He threatened to sue the shop."

"Has he?"

"No."

"What do you think? Was it real or was it a fake?"

"I'd put my money on Barbara. The buyer, his name is Henry, is not a wealthy man. He wears tattered clothes, drives a twenty year old car, and scrimps on everything so he can buy Tiffany pieces. It's almost as if he's obsessed with the objects. I can understand why if someone told him it was a fake, he'd be furious. That's a lot of money to spend for something that's not authentic."

"How did Barbara end the conversation with him?"

"She asked him to give her the name of the appraiser, but he refused to tell her. She told him to have the appraiser call her after tomorrow, because she was going to a local spa for a couple of days. Barbara really wasn't all that concerned about it. She told me that a lot of appraisers these days take a couple of classes in antiques and then call themselves appraisers. It's not a closely regulated occupation. Henry just wanted someone to tell him it was an authentic Tiffany lamp, so Barbara was sure he'd gotten the appraisal from some individual who called himself an appraiser, but had no established credentials."

"Interesting. Does Henry seem like the type of man who could commit a crime?"

"I've only met him once. He's rather fanatical, but whether or not that means he's capable of committing a crime, I don't know. Why?"

"Well, if it's determined that Barbara was murdered, then I would be interested in knowing who might have had a motive for killing her, harsh as that sounds. This guy Henry might fit into that category."

"I see what you mean. I don't think there's anything else I can tell you. I'm going to close the shop and go home. I need to make some decisions about what I need to do now that Barbara is deceased."

"You've been very helpful, Linda. Here's my card. Think about everything we've talked about, and if you remember something you think may be important in helping me understand how and why Barbara died, I'd really appreciate it if you would call me. Thanks, and again, I'm sorry for your loss."

CHAPTER SIX

On the drive back to the spa, Liz looked at the clock on the van's dashboard and realized she'd have to hurry to get the appetizers and dinner made in time for the spa guests. She began to mentally plan what she could fix.

Thank heavens I always keep some appetizers in the freezer that I can heat up in a couple of minutes. Those onion bites and the cheese sausage balls I saved from last week will be perfect. People always love them. No one needs to know they came from the freezer. For dinner I can do a Caesar salad with a make-it-yourself kind of soft taco. I'll fry some onions, peppers, and flap steak, and put it in bowls people can pass around. With cheese, chopped onions, sour cream, and avocado slices, the tacos will seem like the best gourmet Mexican food the guests have ever had. This is definitely a Mexican dinner, so the chocolate mousse I made yesterday with Mexican chocolate will finish it off. Think I'll put a bowl of chopped cooked bacon on the table and the more adventurous ones can sprinkle some on their mousse. Topped with bacon, it's one of my favorite things.

She had just gotten out of her van and was walking into the lodge when her cell phone began to ring. She looked at the screen and saw it was Roger. "Hi Roger. How are you?"

"Finishing up preparing for a trial I've got that starts tomorrow. It looks like it's going to take up the next week or two, so if you don't mind, I thought I'd come up tonight and spend the night. Do you have an empty cottage I can use? I know it's short notice, but I really

26

miss you."

The thought of an empty cottage made her think of Barbara dying in cottage #6. "I'd love it if you could come up. I really would like to talk to you about some things that happened here today. Actually, it's more in your area of expertise than mine."

"Why don't you fill me in now and I can think about them on the way up?"

She quickly told him everything that had happened beginning with when Bertha had burst through the door that morning and concluding with her visit to the antique shop.

"Good grief, Liz. I really don't like this. The police chief sounds like a bumbling idiot. I'll spend the night and leave early tomorrow morning. I can get out of here within the hour. What time do you serve dinner to the guests?"

"I usually have wine and appetizers at 6:30, and I serve dinner at 7:15. That gives them a little time to read or whatever after dinner. As you know, I don't have a television in any of the cottages or in the main lodge, although I do have one in my living quarters. I want them to relax, and the grim news of the day that always seems to be on television sure doesn't help put them in a relaxation mood."

"That's perfect. Plan on me for dinner, and I'll see you about 6:00 unless the traffic gods are working against me."

"Drive safely."

*****

Promptly at 6:00 Liz's cell phone rang. "Hi, Roger, where are you?" she asked, seeing his name pop on her cell phone screen.

"I'm driving up the lane. Just wanted you to know that I made it safe and sound and on time."

While she was still on the phone with him, she walked to the front door of the lodge and opened it, stepping over Brandy Boy, who barely acknowledged her. She saw Roger's dark blue Audi driving up the lane, pressed the end button on her phone, and waved to him. He parked in the lodge parking lot, got out of his car, and walked over to her, giving her a big hug.

"What did I ever do to deserve that?" she asked, laughing. "Actually, I think I could get used to it. It's nice to have a man around and particularly an attractive one."

"Flattery will get you anywhere, ma'am. Keep it up," he said. He opened the trunk of his car and took a small suitcase and bag from it. "Which cottage am I going to be in?" he asked as they walked into the lodge. Without giving it much thought, Liz made a sudden decision.

"Actually, Roger, I think you can put your things downstairs in my living quarters, if that's all right with you," she said shyly.

"All right with me? Are you kidding? I've been hoping against hope that someday this might happen. Are you sure?" he asked, cupping her chin in his hand and kissing her.

"Roger," she said, pulling back and looking up at him. "I've never told you about my niggle. It's kind of this thing I've had all my life and I pretty much listen to it. When I was a little kid it told me not to go down the driveway on my bike. I went anyway. The brake on my bike failed, and I crashed in the middle of the street. A car was racing down the street and came to a screeching halt just inches from me. If I'd listened to my little niggle that near tragedy would never have happened.

"When I was in high school I was the president of our church's youth group and one day we went hiking in the mountains. I got separated from the rest of the group and came to a fork in the trail. I was hopelessly lost and didn't know which way to go. It was late in the day and the weather was rapidly turning bad. If I'd had to spend the night alone in the mountains, I would have been in serious trouble. This thing I call a niggle told me to go down the trail on the left and I did. Sure enough, in a few minutes I saw the group I was with a little farther down the trail. I don't know what would have happened to me if I'd gone down the other trail. I probably wouldn't be here today. Anyway, the niggle is telling me that it would like you to stay with me tonight. Okay?"

"Oh yeah, Liz, oh yeah! I just hope this means what I think it does."

"It does," she said, looking down, her cheeks clearly becoming red.

"I want to make a promise to you. If at any time you want to renege on your decision, I'll understand, and it will be fine with me. Okay?"

"Yes, but the niggle tells me I'm making the right decision. Anyway, I have to get dinner ready for the guests. We can talk after they leave and go back to their cottages. I'd like your thoughts on what I told you about earlier."

"Better get a notepad," Roger said. "I've got a lot to say on the subject and a lot of things I'd like you to do, because this bumbling idiot who calls himself the chief of police sure isn't going to do them. If the autopsy report comes back that Barbara was murdered, you've got to find out who did it in order to protect the reputation of the spa. We'll talk later. I'm going down and unpack. Is this going to be a problem for the guests, you know, me staying in your suite?"

"If it was the people from town then yes, it would be a problem. I'd definitely become the rumor of the moment at Gertie's Diner, but here I don't think the guests will even notice or, for that matter, even care. There's no reason for them to know, and think about it this way, they're only here for a couple of days. They really don't care what the owner of the lodge and spa does in her personal life. Plus, because you're here before they arrive at 6:30, they'll have no idea what cottage you're in. It will be our little secret," she said.

"Well in that case I'll make it a point to be back up here before they arrive. Sure don't want to see your reputation tarnished because of me."

She smiled at him, realizing once again how attractive he was. On someone else the grey that showed on his temples would signal the onset of an aging man, but Roger's salt and pepper hair merely made him look distinguished. His sky blue eyes had permanent crinkle marks next to them from the smile he wore so easily, and she couldn't deny that she was looking forward to becoming familiar with a body that definitely showed signs of being well taken care of.

"Back in a minute, sweetheart," he said. "I need to get out of this courtroom suit and into something a little more comfortable."

"I'd go with you, but I really need to get ready for my guests, and Roger, thanks for coming on such short notice."

"Actually, Liz, it's probably better if you don't come downstairs with me. We might be late for your guests, and that could be both embarrassing as well as bad for business."

"You're incorrigible!" she laughed, throwing a dish towel at him.

CHAPTER SEVEN

After dinner and when the last guest had left the lodge, Roger said, "Liz, I'll be back in a minute. I made some notes concerning what I think you should do if it turns out that the woman who died in cottage #6 didn't die of natural causes. They're downstairs."

She took the last of the chocolate mousse bowls from the dinner table, rinsed them, and put them in the dishwasher. Bertha would be coming in to get the breakfast ready for the guests in the morning, but Liz didn't want her to walk into the kitchen and find dirty dishes left from the evening meal. Liz treasured Bertha and knew that part of the success of the spa was due to the seamless way she handled everything associated with it. Liz had come to rely on her, but just as importantly, she considered her to be a friend.

Liz always prepared a couple of different casseroles for Bertha to heat for the guests' breakfast. When Bertha came to the lodge in the mornings she assembled a buffet style breakfast table for the guests, so they could help themselves to the casseroles as well as croissants, butter, jam, bagels, a large bowl of fresh fruit, and hot tea or coffee. Each morning, as Bertha turned to drive up the lane that led to the lodge, she stopped at the mailbox and picked up the San Francisco Chronicle and the Portland Tribune for the guests. They helped themselves to breakfast, and many stayed long after they'd eaten, reading the morning newspapers.

She put the last of the dishes in the dishwasher and had just started it when Roger returned. "Why don't you sit down, Liz. I brought you a notepad and a pen. I have some thoughts and ideas."

They sat at the large cedar dining room table, and Roger began to speak. "Let's assume that the autopsy shows that the woman, I think you said her name was Barbara, died of natural causes. If that's so, then you really don't need to do anything. I'm sure it will be in the local newspaper, and you probably know the editor. I would call him and tell him how sorry you are this happened at the spa, and all that kind of feel-good stuff. However, if the report comes back that she didn't die of natural causes, meaning that she was murdered, I think you should say you're going to do everything you can to find out who murdered her. From what you've told me, that bumbling police chief is probably incapable of solving the crime, so it would only make sense for you to do everything you can to solve the crime and protect the reputation of the spa."

"Roger, do you really think Barbara could have been murdered? It just doesn't seem possible for something like that to happen in our sleepy little town of Red Cedar."

"I don't know, but after thirty years of practicing criminal law, not much surprises me. I want you to start thinking like one of the private investigators I use. I really wish I could be here to help you, but the trial I'm starting tomorrow has already been delayed twice, and there is no way the judge will grant another continuance."

"Okay, I'm ready. Shoot."

"I always approach a case from the standpoint of who has the most to gain if the person is dead. Usually the first person I look at is the spouse, if there is one. You told me there was a good chance Barbara's spouse was having an affair. So I would start by asking myself if he would want to kill his wife, so he could be with the woman he was having an affair with. You also told me her husband had just been re-elected as mayor, and that there were some damaging accusations made against him during the election campaign. Who was his opponent? Was Barbara's murder a vendetta possibly committed by someone wanting to get back at the husband by killing her? I'd take a long look at any relative or spouse of his opponent. I'd talk to the editor of the paper and ask him on what facts he based the accusations printed in the paper. Maybe the mayor had some hidden baggage and someone wanted to kill his wife because of that. Maybe the mayor knew something, and someone had threatened that if he didn't keep quiet, his wife would be killed. I know it sounds like I'm talking about some real longshots here, but I'm looking for anything that might lead to identifying the killer. I've found that one thing always leads to another."

"I can't believe someone would kill over a lost election."

"You're being naïve. People will kill over anything and often do," Roger said. "So at this point we've identified two possible suspects. Let's start by taking a look at the antique store situation, which I find very interesting. Barbara's partner doesn't seem to have anything to gain by Barbara being dead if what she says is true about her being the money behind the shop and Barbara being what I would call the front woman. Barbara knew everybody in the area and was an expert in a specific style of antiques, but did Barbara's partner tell you the truth? Perhaps Barbara and she both put in an equal amount of money, and if Barbara's dead, she gets it all. Maybe they really were legal partners and the shop was in both of their names. I can help you with getting information about the ownership of the store. Sean, one of my private investigators, can do a computer search and easily find that kind of information."

"That would be great. I wouldn't know how or where to begin."

"Trust me, it's not that big a deal. City records would have all that information. It's pretty easy to find those records. Let's go on. Then there's the antique guy who threatened to sue her over the Tiffany lamp. You should probably take a close look at him. Since he lives in San Francisco, I'll have Sean look into that as well. Shouldn't be too difficult. I imagine he's well-known in the antique world. Sean can check out that angle."

"I'm totally new at this," Liz said, "but the person I wondered about from the beginning is Darcy, the high school principal who was at Dave's house when I went there. She's the one Seth, the police chief, mentioned was having an affair with Dave. Maybe she wants to marry Dave. Don't forget Linda, the antique store person, told me Barbara was a very strong Catholic and wouldn't divorce Dave. I think Darcy should be investigated."

"Couldn't agree more. Now you're starting to think like a private eye. You told me once that Gertie's Diner was the hotbed for rumors in town. You might want to go there and see if you can find out anything. If they were having an affair, someone there probably knows about it."

"I'll go there tomorrow."

"You mentioned Barbara had a facial and a massage yesterday, and from what you told me, it sure didn't sound like the police chief did a very thorough job of investigating that angle, although I think it's kind of a stretch. I can't come up with a motive either one of the spa employees might have had to kill Barbara, but believe me, I know for a fact that stranger things have happened."

"Judy's coming up and we'd planned on getting some treatments. I think I'll book a treatment with each of those two women, and it would be a very natural thing to talk about it, if, in fact, it turns out she was murdered. Roger, the thing that really scares me is the bad publicity the spa will get if she was murdered. I don't know how I can get around that."

"You can't, and that's why you need to do everything you can to find out who killed Barbara if she was murdered. The faster you can do that, the less time the press will have to make a big deal of it."

"If she didn't die of natural causes, I assume the coroner will be able to pin down the exact cause of death."

"Yes, he should be able to make that determination, but what if she died from a combination of sleeping pills and alcohol? That wouldn't necessarily mean that she committed suicide, it just means that was the cause of death. Maybe someone slipped a foreign substance in something she drank or forced her to drink it. That's where it gets difficult and interesting, and that's why it's important to find out who might have had a motive to kill her. Once you get a list of the people who might have had a motive for seeing her dead you'll need to find out where each of those people was at the time she was murdered."

Liz nervously ran her fingers through her hair. "I have no idea how I can find out all the things you've just mentioned. I just hope that the coroner determines she died from natural causes."

"For your sake and the sake of the spa, I hope so too, but you need to be prepared for the alternative. Liz, people trust you and like you, and you're one of those people who is very easy to talk to. I think that's one reason you've made such a success of the spa. Just do what comes naturally. Talk to people. You'll find out what you need to know in the natural flow of things. Anyway, enough about Barbara. I have to get up very early, and it's time for bed. Have any second doubts?" he asked, taking her hand in his.

"No, I feel as sure about this as I have about anything in a long time."

"Good. Look at it this way. We're two older people who, I believe, have come to care deeply about each other. Let's see where it goes. This is new territory for both of us."

CHAPTER EIGHT

"Good morning, beautiful. I hope you slept as well as I did. Stay where you are," Roger said as he swung his long legs out of bed and stood up. "It's too early for you to get up, but I have to get on the road in case I hit some traffic going into the city. I'm hoping it's early enough I can avoid it, and I could use a couple more hours of pre-trial work."

"Absolutely not," Liz answered. "I'm getting up and making you coffee. I made some sweet rolls for this morning's guest breakfast, so you can take a couple of those on the road with you. I'll even give you a bunch of napkins so you don't spill on your go to court suit that you'll be wearing."

"If you insist. While you're making coffee, I'll shower and shave. There's something else I want to tell you when you come back."

A few minutes later she walked into the bathroom with a cup of coffee in each hand. Roger had wrapped a towel around his waist and stood in front of the mirror, shaving.

"I put your sweet rolls in a container, but I thought you'd probably want the coffee now. I also have a travel cup you can take with you for when you're on the road. What did you want to tell me?"

"I was going to tell you last night, but I got sidetracked," he said, looking over at her and smiling. He turned back to the mirror and resumed shaving. "I have a friend who trains guard dogs. The police buy their dogs from him as well as private individuals, particularly men who travel a lot and want to feel that their families are safe while they're away. I called him yesterday afternoon after I talked to you. I told him I wanted to buy one as a gift for someone who had a large piece of property and a lot of people coming and going. I told him the dog had to be non-threatening unless the owner gave an appropriate command to the dog. I asked him if he currently had any dogs that fit that description, and he told me he had just completed training a dog that perfectly fit into that category. The dog is a nine month old large fawn colored male boxer.

"My friend told me he's so good with people that he's been taking him home at night to play with his children, but he said the dog was trained to obey commands to attack or guard. He said the dog could take a two hundred fifty pound man to the ground in a matter of seconds and hold him there until the release command was given by the dog's owner. He also said the dog's deep growl alone was enough to stop most intruders. I asked him if a woman could handle the dog, and he said most of the people who bought that particular breed were women, because the breed isn't as frightening looking as say a bull mastiff or a doberman pinscher."

"I think I know where this is going," Liz said.

"If you thought that my friend would be delivering a dog by the name of Winston to you, you'd be right. I know how much you love Brandy Boy, but let's be honest, a guard dog he is not." He turned away from the mirror and faced her again. "Liz, after I talked to you yesterday afternoon, I really became concerned for your personal safety given the somewhat remote location of the spa. This is a big piece of property with a lot of people coming and going. If the woman's death isn't murder, you'll just have a nice guard dog for the property. If it was murder, you'll have protection with you at all times. I'd really like you to take the dog with you everywhere you go. It sure would make me feel a lot better if you agree to accept my gift."

"Actually I've been thinking about getting a guard dog. I agree that Brandy Boy is a wonderful dog, but guarding and protecting is not his thing. Since I've been living alone, I'm much more aware of the night sounds. Yes, I accept your gift, although I imagine it was pretty pricey. Thank you, Roger. Did you and your friend set up a time for me to meet Winston?"

"Yes. I know I was acting presumptively, but this is really important to me. I know I don't have the right to insist that you do anything, but I was hoping against hope it would be okay with you. He told me he'd be here about noon today unless I called him and told him you'd refused the dog. He told me to tell you you'll need a dog bed, a leash, and some dog food. He said Winston eats anything, so whatever kind of dog food you get will be fine. Winston is fully housebroken and trained not to chew on things other than his own toys, but he did suggest you might want to get a couple of chew toys, just in case."

"Well, I was going to Gertie's Diner this morning to see if I can learn anything at the local rumor mill, so I can get whatever I need when I'm in town. It's been a few years since I've had an active dog. At least the spa property is fenced, other than the section where the cliff leads to the ocean, so I won't have to worry about him running away.

"Liz, this dog will be better trained than probably any of our adult children. He not only is trained to protect and guard, but my friend makes sure that all of the other basic commands are covered in his training. About the only thing you'll have to do is open your home and your heart to him."

"It's thawing. As you can probably tell, it's definitely thawing," she said smiling. "Well, didn't know when I woke up a half hour ago I'd be looking forward to becoming a dog owner. Guess you just never know where the day is going to take you. By the way, you look great. If I was a juror, I'd definitely think the guy wasn't guilty just because the way his attorney looks," she said with a smile on her face and a twinkle in her eye.

"Thanks for the compliment, but it's a little more complicated than that. I have to try and keep this guy out of prison for life."

"Roger, is it ever hard for you? I mean, there must be times that you know in your heart of hearts the guy you're defending is guilty. Isn't that difficult for you?"

"No. From the time I graduated from law school and decided to go into criminal law to and through this moment, the one thing I've held sacred is that every person accused of a crime is not guilty unless proven so. It's my job to make sure that no one proves my clients guilty, and over the last thirty years my track record is pretty good, but your question is one I get asked a lot. I'd love to stay, but I've got to get on the road."

She walked him out to where his car was parked, noticing that the spa and all of the cabin lights were off. "Doesn't look like I have any early birds this morning. Sometimes the guests who are really 'Type A's' are already jogging this early in the morning. Personally, I like to break gently into the day. Good luck and I'll call you tonight with the autopsy results."

He put his suitcase and bag in the trunk and turned towards her, wrapping her in his arms. "Last night was one of the most special nights of my life. I won't forget a moment of it. Thank you." He kissed her and got in his car.

"Be safe," she said, as he put the car in gear and began his drive back to the city.

Well, my life sure has turned upside down in the last twenty-four hours. Let's see, a possible murder, a man who is suddenly more than just a good friend, and a new dog. Couldn't have predicted this in a million years, but other than the murder, I sure like the other two.

CHAPTER NINE

"Hi, honey. Good to see you. What brings you to town this morning?" Gertie asked. Liz looked up from her menu and couldn't help but smile. She thought if someone drew a caricature of a woman who owned a place called Gertie's Diner, it would look exactly like the woman standing in front of her, from her dyed bottle blond hair worn in a beehive style that had been popular in the 1960's, to her four inch high heels. She had a habit of chewing bubble gum and blowing big pink bubbles, but she was blessed with a heart as big as gold. You only had to come to Gertie's once, and from then on, you were her friend for life.

"Heard there was a little excitement out at your spa yesterday. Seth and Leroy were telling everyone in hearin' distance how Barbara Nelson bit the dust. Said she died from an overdose of sleeping pills and booze. Any truth to that?"

"Gertie, that's not a fact. Wes is doing the autopsy today, and as of now no one knows the exact cause of her death. They really shouldn't have said anything, but I'm not surprised considering the source."

"You ain't kiddin' about that. Those two yokels don't have enough smarts between them to get out of the rain. Seth was playin' it up to the hilt when he was here. Everyone was hangin' on every word the two of them said. I suppose it made 'em feel real important, but it's a fact we don't have many suicides 'round these parts. Makes me kinda' wonder if those two bozos know what they're jawin' about. Seth said she did it cuz' she found out Darcy and Dave were having an affair, but lawdy, everyone knows that's not the first time Dave's been visiting another henhouse. Beats me why she'd do it now. What do you think?"

"I don't have enough information to make a guess and until Wes releases the autopsy report, I think everyone should keep their opinions to themselves. If Dave was having an affair with Darcy do you think he wanted to leave Barbara and marry Darcy?"

"From what I hear, and it's only what I hear, Darcy would do anything to get Dave to marry her. She's gettin' a little long in the tooth to be very marriageable even if she is a looker, and the pickins' are pretty slim 'round here. Now it looks like she'll get what she wants."

"To change the subject, the man who ran against Dave. Darn. I can never remember his name."

"Think you'd remember it cuz' the handyman you got workin' out at the spa's his brother. Name's Gene Harris. Kinda too bad he lost the election. That's the third time he's lost to Dave. Bound to make a body mad. Hear Zack was at his brother's on election night, got drunk, and a coupla their friends had to keep him from going over to Dave's victory party and beatin' him up. Don't know for sure. Just heard it. You know, I hear a lot of things in this 'ol diner. Some true, and I'm sure some not."

"I didn't know Gene and Zack were brothers. Zack does a great job for me. He's been working at the spa ever since we bought it, and I've never had any problems with him."

"Like I said, never know for sure if what I'm hearin' is true. Tell you one other little rumor I picked up on yesterday. Heard that Dave was going to sue Bart over at the Trib for libel because he wrote those editorials hintin' that Dave was takin' city funds. Course like everything else, don't know what's true. Always felt like Barbara was the one who kept Dave from actin' up. We'll see what happens now."

"Do you know if Dave's going to have a funeral for her?"

"Sakes alive, of course he is. Dave wouldn't miss a chance to have all of Red Cedar pay homage to him, even if it was his wife that died. Yeah, there's gonna be a big funeral at St. Isadore's Catholic Church. That's the church Barbara attended and then she's going to be buried in the town cemetery. Gonna be a big reception at the Elks Lodge followin' the burial. From what I've been hearin' this mornin', it's gonna be a pretty big deal. Drove of Does is gonna' prepare all the food."

"The Drove of Does? I've never heard that term. Who or what is it?"

"Those are the wives of the Elks' lodge members. It's a woman's organization that helps the lodge members when they have a party or a big event. We got a lot of Does around these parts. They kind of like belongin' to somethin', and the bartender over at the Lodge pours a mighty stiff drink. Course I'm sure the Does never imbibe," she said, winking. "I've been jawin' too long. What can I get you?"

"I'd like a chocolate malted milk. Can't justify a hamburger this early, but I don't think there's a special time for malted milks. They're always good."

"Back in a sec, honey." She and her high heels tottered off to the kitchen while Liz said a silent prayer that she wouldn't fall on her way.

Liz pulled her phone out of her purse to see if she'd had any calls. She had her head down looking at it when she heard a voice that made her want to retch.

"Well, lookee here. If it ain't my lucky day. So little lady, got any black lace on today?" the fat jowly faced police chief asked as he tried to work his belly into the booth opposite of her.

"I'll pretend I didn't hear that, Seth. Have you heard anything from Wes about the results of the autopsy?"

"Nah, usually takes him a few hours for him to cut 'em up. Think he gets his jollies from it, if you know what I mean," Seth said in a suggestive voice. "Anyway, glad yer' here. Gettin' some reports that Zack Harris has been making noises 'bout knockin' Dave's head around. Ya' know anything about that?"

"No. I didn't even know until a little while ago that Gene and Zack were brothers. I don't schedule the employees' time off, but I think Bertha mentioned something about Zack taking a little vacation time before we got real busy during the summer season. I haven't seen him for several days."

"Well is that so? Guess I'll have to keep an eye out fer him. By the way, jes' got me a new Victoria's Secret catalog delivered in the mail yesterday. Seen a coupla things that got yer name on 'em and I circled 'em. Uh-oh, Leroy jes' stuck his head in the door. Probably lookin' fer me. When I get them VC things, I'd like a private showin, if ya' know what I mean." As Seth tried to slide out of the booth, Liz wasn't sure who was going to win the battle over Seth's stomach, the table or him. Ultimately he won and was able to free himself and get out of the booth. "Be seein' ya soon I hope, pretty lady," the grossly obese police chief said, oblivious to how ridiculous he looked and acted.

I feel like I need a shower after I'm around him. If it turns out Barbara didn't die of natural causes, I'm definitely going to have to do whatever I can to clear the spa's name. If Seth can't get his belly out of a booth, I doubt if he could ever solve a murder, she thought.

CHAPTER TEN

As Liz turned onto the lane that led to the lodge she noticed a large SUV turning in right behind her. She looked at the clock on her dashboard and realized it was almost noon. *Uh-oh*, she thought, *I got carried away talking to Gertie and stayed too long at the diner. I'll bet that SUV belongs to Roger's friend. Don't think Roger would be very happy with me if I'd blown the appointment, particularly after he went to so much trouble for me and the guy drove all the way up from San Francisco.*

She pulled up to the lodge and couldn't help but smile as she looked at the simple rustic building made of wood and glass standing before her. Brightly colored plants and tubs of blooming flowers stood in stark contrast to the green forest and blue Pacific Ocean in the background.

There's nowhere else in the world I would want to live, not that I've ever been anywhere else in the world. I remember how I used to tell Joe we needed to travel and visit some foreign countries. He always refused, using the excuse that he couldn't leave his auto dealerships for that long. Now that I probably could go somewhere once in a while, I have absolutely no desire to leave here. Everything I want is here and now with the addition of Roger in my life, I have more of a reason to stay here. Even with Barbara's death, I still think I'm one of the luckiest people in the world to be living right here in Red Cedar!

Lost in her momentary reverie, she hadn't noticed that a man had gotten out of the SUV and was walking over to her van. She opened the door and greeted him. "Hi, I'm Liz Lucas. You must be Roger's friend."

The tall lanky man dressed in jeans and a leather jacket with his white hair tied in a ponytail smiled warmly at her, extended his hand, and said, "I'm Ed James, and I've brought you a new little friend. Well, actually he's not so little. Are you ready to be introduced to him?"

"This was a huge surprise to me, but yes, I think I'm ready. I've never had a boxer before, so you'll have to give me some guidelines on how to handle him."

"His name is Winston. I've had him since he was eight weeks old. I don't know if Roger told you, but I've been taking him home with me after work. My three boys love him, and they really wanted to keep him. My wife put her foot down, saying that five dogs were more than enough."

"You have five dogs and three boys? Good grief, I don't blame her. Should Winston and I meet out here or in the lodge?"

"Right here is fine. After you're introduced we'll go in the lodge. He's completely housebroken and trained." He walked over to the SUV and opened the rear door. "Winston, come."

Liz's breath caught in her throat as she looked at the beautiful boxer jumping out of the SUV. He had four white stocking feet and a blaze of white on his face, along with a full white collar. She bent down and put out her hand. Winston walked over to her, sat, and licked her hand. He held out his paw to her and they shook. She looked up at Ed. "He is just beautiful. I can't believe he wanted to shake hands with me."

"Along with training my dogs as guard and attack dogs, I like to teach them some tricks. Dogs like Winston look pretty threatening to children, so when a child can make them do tricks, they aren't so afraid of them. Let's go in the lodge. You can tell him to follow you."

"Winston, follow," Liz said. Winston stood next to Liz and walked into the lodge with them, ignoring Brandy Boy who was asleep on the porch. "Would you like a cup of coffee, Ed? I can make some in just a few minutes."

"No thanks. I have a couple of other deliveries to make today, so I need to get back. I've written out a list of commands you can use for Winston. Roger mentioned you own the lodge and the spa. He said you had living quarters of your own below the lodge. Is that where you plan on having Winston sleep?"

"Yes. I put his bed down there, and I also bought another one. Do you think it would be all right if I put the other dog bed over there in the corner of the great room?"

"Liz, let's be honest. Winston is here because he's primarily a guard dog who will be guarding you. Yes, he knows tricks, but that's not why Roger wanted you to have him. He wanted to make sure you were protected at all times, however, if Winston isn't with you, he can't protect you. I can see from just driving in here that this property is an invitation to someone thinking about committing a crime. Anyone could enter this property.

"You have a fence, but it's more of a fence that enhances the looks of the property rather than being a fence built for protection. I'm certain, given the nature of your business, that an electric fence is not an option, nor is a gate at the property entrance that would have to be unlocked. I'm also sure your guests need to feel free to come and go as they please, and it would probably frighten some of them if they had to pass through a locked gate. Quite frankly, living here on your own, I'm rather surprised there aren't some types of security devices in place for your protection. Things like motion activated exterior floodlights or a video security camera would be something you might want to consider having installed."

"When my husband was alive, I never thought about it. I have a handyman who's here during the day, but at night there are just the guests and me. I suppose a deranged guest could stay here, but I've never had any problems. In all honesty, I have thought about getting a dog for protection, but I never got around to it. I'm sure you saw the St. Bernard asleep on the porch. Obviously he's not much protection. I have to admit I'm glad Roger took care of it."

"I don't know what your relationship is with Roger, but he must care a great deal about you to buy one of the dogs I train. Believe me, they don't come cheap. My business supports my family, and I have a reputation on the West Coast as being the number one trainer of guard dogs. I met Roger years ago when he needed me to testify as an expert witness in one of his cases. A woman had been attacked by a man's dog and she was suing him. I was able to show that she had antagonized the dog and his client walked away from the lawsuit. Roger and I have been friends ever since. He's a good man. He took the death of his wife pretty hard. In fact, it darned near destroyed him. Work was his salvation, but it looks like he may have found another salvation," Ed said with a twinkle in his eye and an easy smile on his face.

"In all honesty, I don't know any more than you do about what my relationship with Roger is, but I will tell you this, I like him a lot and yes, like you said, he is a good man. Thanks for telling me that." She bent down and scratched Winston behind his ears. "Well, boy, it's you and me. Brandy Boy's here, but that doesn't mean much. Say goodbye to Ed, and then I'll give you the grand tour."

"Winston, come," Ed said, kneeling. "You take care of Liz. You're a good boy, and I'm going to miss you. Stay." He stood up and turned towards the door, but not before Liz saw that his eyes were a little too shiny. She was pretty certain it was from unshed tears.

"Ed, thanks for taking the time to deliver Winston to me. I promise he'll have a good home, and I also promise we'll pay you a visit in a few months."

He walked down the steps to the SUV and gave her a half wave. Seconds later he was gone.

Liz spent the next hour showing Winston the lodge, her living quarters, the spa, the cottages, and ended where the lane met the highway. She'd glanced at the sheet of instructions Ed had given her. On it he'd written that if there was an area where she didn't want Winston to go, she should use the words, "No go." The only thing that had concerned her about Winston's safety was the highway at the end of the lane. It was fairly busy and she was worried that Winston might go onto it and get hit by a car. When they reached the end of the lane, she turned to him, took his head in her hands and looked directly at him. "Winston, no go. No go." She put her foot on the highway and repeated the command. He backed up, and she could swear he understood exactly what she was telling him and why she was telling him. They turned and began the short walk back to the lodge, a happy dog and a happy new dog owner.

*****

Just before they reached the lodge, she heard the noise of a car engine coming from behind them on the lane, and she stepped to the side and stopped. "Winston, come. Sit." Winston instantly sat and looked up at her expectantly, waiting for his next command.

"Hey, Mrs. Lucas. Got a new dog?"

She turned and looked at the man behind the wheel of the run-down rusted truck. It was Zack, and it was obvious from his appearance that he hadn't paid any attention to his grooming for a couple of days. She didn't know what he'd been doing during his short vacation, but it didn't appear to be anything health-related. His hazel eyes were bloodshot, and he obviously hadn't shaved for several days as there was far more than a five o'clock shadow on his face. His sandy colored hair looked like it hadn't been washed for a long time, and his shirt was covered with food spots and what she suspected were beer stains.

"Hi Zack. How was your vacation? And yes, this is Winston. I just got him."

"Scary looking, but he's a beauty. As for my vacation? Not so good. Don't know if you knew that my brother was the one who was running against Dave Nelson for mayor. He's run twice before against Dave, and once again, he lost. Losing wouldn't be so bad, but what's tough is that he had to lose to that man. He's as dirty as they come. Just can't prove it. Got Bart over at the Red Cedar Trib to write a couple of pieces about Dave, but I just came from his office and he told me he won't be writing any more articles. Something about getting sued by Dave for character assassination. Said he didn't have any hard evidence that Dave had ever done anything wrong. Looks like that snake in the grass covered his tracks, that's for sure."

"I'm sorry your brother lost, but I really haven't been involved in the city elections."

"Well, I wouldn't bother. It's obvious people don't think when they vote or worse yet, don't even want to know the facts. Guy has so much dirt on him he'd need a case of bleach to get himself clean. Cheats on everything from his wife to his taxes. Understand his wife died in one of the cottages here. Too bad it wasn't him."

"Zack, that's pretty harsh. I don't think that's something you want to say publicly! If someone hears you say that, they're going to want to know where you were when she died, and right now we don't even know what happened to her."

"Seth says she called it quits 'cuz of the affair that slimy husband of hers was having with Darcy Martinez and as far as where I was, I have no idea. Got to drinking a little too much on my vacation 'cuz my brother lost the election, and things are a little hazy. I'm feeling much better today and ready to get back to work. Anything special you need me to do?"

"Can't think of anything offhand, but you better check with Bertha."

"Think I better start planting some flowers I bought before my vacation. I've got a bunch of empty pots I can get them going in, because in a few weeks all the ones we have next to the cottages and on the steps of the spa and lodge are going to need to be replaced."

"Thanks Zack. That sounds good. I love the flowers. They're a nice contrast to the forest and the ocean. Tourist season is just around the corner, and we're always booked solid in the summer. See you later."

"Think it's a good thing you got a little protection for yourself with that dog. Strange things can happen at a place like this," he said as he started the truck and drove it towards the lodge parking area.

That's a weird thing to say. Wonder where he was during the night and in the early morning hours yesterday. Actually, I hope it won't be necessary to find out. I'm hoping against hope Barbara died from natural causes. It sure would make my life and everyone else's a lot easier if that was the case.

CHAPTER ELEVEN

"Okay, Winston. You've had the grand tour of your new home. The only thing I haven't done is give you the tour of the van, but I think that can wait until we actually go somewhere. For now, why don't you lie down and get comfortable while I check the messages on the answerphone."

So it's come to this. I must be getting old. I'm actually enjoying conversing with a dog.

Liz decided when she and Joe bought the lodge and spa that Bertha would handle the reservations for the cottages. After taking a reservation for a cottage, Bertha would transfer the guest to the spa receptionist who would set up their spa treatments. Liz hadn't wanted to get bogged down taking these types of reservations. One of the main reasons she'd wanted to buy the lodge and spa was so she could cook the family style meals that were served to the guests. She'd always loved to cook and entertain and Joe had pridefully maintained that she was one of the reasons his car dealerships had been so successful. When they lived in the San Francisco area they'd entertained clients and friends weekly at her infamous dinner parties, and she'd always enjoyed it. The only difference at the spa was that every night there was a different cast of characters, all with a different story, a story she was a master at getting them to tell. Meeting the people, cooking, and making their stay at the Red Cedar Spa memorable was something she enjoyed every minute of the day.

With almost all of the spa reservations and calls going through Bertha, she knew when she saw the blinking red light on the answerphone it meant a message had been left, and it was probably a personal one for her. She also knew it wasn't her daughter, Brittany, or her son, Jonah, since they always called her on her cell phone. While she was of an older generation that still relied on land lines, her children definitely were not. Their cell phones were as much a part of them as their hands and feet.

She pressed the blinking button to listen to the message while she looked over and smiled at Winston who was fast asleep in his new bed, the stuffed toy she had dubbed Mr. Hedgehog, lying right next to his nose.

"Mrs. Lucas, this is Wes Anderson, the county coroner. I'm afraid I have some bad news. Barbara Nelson did not die of natural causes. It looks like murder, and due to the lack of any signs of a physical struggle or needle punctures indicating that something was injected into her body, my feeling is that she died from something she ate or drank. In other words, she was poisoned. I'm able to do some very basic testing for foreign substances in my lab, and I found no traces of the chemicals found in sleeping pills or the bourbon that was on her nightstand. However, she definitely had some type of a foreign substance in her body, but with my limited testing equipment, I don't have the ability to determine exactly what the substance was that killed her.

"Like I said, I feel certain she was poisoned. I've sent a sample of her blood to the police lab in San Francisco. They usually get back to me pretty fast, so I'm hoping I'll know something by tomorrow or the next day. The problem then becomes, while we may know what killed her, we won't know who killed her or how the poisonous substance was introduced into her body. I don't want to tell you how to run your business, Mrs. Lucas, but you don't have to be a psychic to understand that having this happen at the Red Cedar Spa is not going to be good for your business. Word will be out shortly because I have to tell the police chief, and he suffers from a severe case of diarrhea of the mouth. Rather imagine it will be all over town in a few hours. As bumbling as he is, if he can solve it, and that's a big if, it will probably be later rather than sooner. My advice is to see what you can find out on your own. If you have any questions, feel free to call me."

Liz listened to the message for a second time, not fully comprehending what the coroner was saying. Stunned by the disclosure, she sat for a moment, trying to digest the enormity of what he had said.

So Barbara was murdered. She didn't die of natural causes, and she didn't commit suicide. The coroner thinks she was poisoned but doesn't know by what or by whom. Word will soon be all over town, and the spa will get a huge black eye unless I can find out who did it. I've never done anything like this, and I don't know where to begin. About the only thing I have is my little niggle and Winston, but I have no idea if that will be enough. Uh-oh, I better find out if the coroner told Dave. If not, I better be the one to tell him. I'd hate for him to go into Gertie's and find out from someone that the police chief had already been there and shot off his big mouth to anyone who would listen. Like Roger said, the spouse is usually the first suspect in a murder case.

She called Wes back. "Wes, this is Liz Lucas. I got your message. I have one question, well, actually two. Have you told Seth yet, and have you told Dave?" She listened and then said, "Would you do me a favor and wait about an hour before you tell Seth? I'd like to tell Dave myself, and I'd also like to ask him where he was from the time Barbara left the lodge after dinner at about 8:30 until the time when Bertha found her a little after 8:00 the next morning. It seems to me there's almost a twelve hour time frame when anyone who is a possible suspect needs to account for their whereabouts. It sounds very strange to me to be using terms like suspects, but I guess I better get used to it if I'm going to solve the crime. By the way, I appreciate your words of advice about me trying to find out who did it, but I have to tell you this is completely new territory for me. Looking at something through the eyes of a private investigator is nothing I've ever done before, but it's something I better try to do if I want to keep my spa's reputation from having mud splattered all over it. When you get the results back from the police lab in San Francisco, I'd really like to know what they found out. Thanks a lot for telling me first about the autopsy results."

After she ended the call she said, "Winston, come. Time for your first trip in the van. We need to go see Dave and tell him his wife was murdered. Just the visit I really want to make. Let's go." She picked up her purse and headed out the front door. As usual, Brandy Boy was sound asleep on the porch. He opened one eye when Liz closed the door, not bothering to acknowledge Winston.

"You're a good rider, Winston," she said a few minutes later. "I'd take you into Dave's house with me, but I don't think I'm in any danger from him. You stay in the van. This shouldn't take long."

She knocked on the front door, and this time it was quickly opened by Dave. "Hello, Liz. I hope you have a more pleasant reason to be here than you did yesterday. Please come in." He looked past her and saw Winston standing on the front seat of the van. "New addition to the family, or have you always had him?"

She walked into the hallway. "A friend gave him to me today. He thought I needed a guard dog out at the spa." She took a deep breath and said, "I wish this was purely a social visit, but I just had a call from Wes Anderson. The autopsy report indicates Barbara was murdered."

She was curious as to what his reaction would be. He bent over as if he'd been punched in the stomach, and said stuttering, "BBaarbara wwwas mmmurdered. That can't be. Wwhho would murder Barbara? WWhhy?" He stumbled to a nearby chair, sat down heavily, and put his head in his hands. "Are you certain?" he asked after a few moments, taking his hands away from his face and looking at her.

If he's acting, he's doing a very good job, but then again, I've never had to tell anyone their wife was murdered, so I really don't know if this is a normal or abnormal reaction to hearing news like that.

"All I know is what Wes told me. He thinks she was poisoned. Wes said he had the necessary testing equipment to determine that she didn't die from an overdose of alcohol or sleeping pills or a combination of the two. He couldn't identify the substance used to poison her because his testing equipment is not state of the art. He didn't see any needle marks on her body, so he assumed she ingested whatever it was orally. He sent a blood sample to the police lab in San Francisco and said he should hear something from them tomorrow or the next day."

"Barbara didn't take drugs of any kind. She wouldn't even take aspirin. I really don't understand this. Someone must have given her something, maybe hiding it in her food or whatever, but who or why?"

"I have no idea. It's been my experience from the little I've had to do with the Red Cedar police chief that solving this case in a timely manner is not going to happen. Since her death occurred on my property, I'm going to ask a few questions of the people who knew her well. Sorry Dave, but any good detective would ask where you were between the hours of 8:30 night before last and 8:00 yesterday morning."

"You're kidding, right? This is ridiculous. I don't have to answer that question. It's none of your business," he said angrily.

"Since it's my reputation that's on the line here, I'm definitely not kidding. If you don't tell me, I may have to ask the state police to come in and investigate, and I don't think either one of us wants that along with the bad publicity that will go with it. I wouldn't think a recently re-elected mayor who might have thoughts of higher office would like that kind of publicity."

He was quiet for a moment with a grim look on his face, seemingly deep in thought. "You met Darcy Martinez when you were here yesterday." He looked down at his hands. "Barbara and I had an agreement. Over the years, we'd lost interest in each other. There just wasn't anything there anymore. We had nothing in common. I was interested in politics. She was interested in antiques. Darcy shared my passion for politics, and in the last few months, we've been seeing one another. I was with her on the night in question, but let me make one thing crystal clear. I respected Barbara and almost put her on a pedestal. She knew about Darcy, but I was very careful to be discreet. I don't think anyone in town even suspects that Darcy and I are seeing one another. As the principal of the high school, she had to protect her reputation as much as I had to as mayor."

This man is living in a dream world. Gertie, the police chief, and everyone else in town seem to know about the affair. What is he thinking?

"Thank you for sharing that with me. I know it must be painful to have to admit something like that, but sometimes in life these things happen. I won't be the one to sully your reputation by telling people about it. I'll leave you alone now. Stay where you are and I'll let myself out. Oh, by the way, where does Darcy live?"

"Why? Are you going to check my story with her?"

"I'd like to know where she was during those hours. Given the circumstances, I'm sure you'll agree that a prudent investigator would want to ask her that question."

"Well, she'll tell you the same thing I just told you. She lives in the apartments across the street from Lucky Boy Supermarket. Her apartment number is 201."

Liz opened the front door and walked down the sidewalk to her van. Winston was wagging his tail, clearly glad she'd returned from possible harm's way, safe and sound.

"Good job guarding the van, Winston. Good boy. I have to make one more stop, and then we'll go home. When we get back to the lodge, I need to call Judy and confirm she's coming up tomorrow. Also, I need to discuss everything that's happened today with Roger. He's going to want to know how I like you, which I really do, and I'd like to know how his trial is going."

A few minutes later Liz pulled up to an attractive brick apartment building with white wooden shutters and brightly colored flower beds flanking the sidewalk that led to the large cedar entry doors. She turned to Winston. "Stay. I'll be back in a few minutes." She entered the building and saw the elevator a few feet down the hall. She took it to the second floor and made her way to apartment 201 which was only a few steps from the elevator. Liz heard music coming from inside the apartment. She knocked on the door, and a few moments later it was opened by Darcy.

She stood there looking at Liz, obviously trying to place her. After a moment she smiled with recognition and said, "Please come in. I met you yesterday at Dave's home. You're the owner of the Red Cedar Spa. I just left the high school. What can I do for you?"

Liz told her what the coroner had said. Darcy stood quietly for a moment, looking out the window, and then she began speaking. "I only met Barbara once, but she seemed very nice. Do you have any idea who might have killed her?"

"No, I wish I did. Since she died on my property, I definitely want to find out who did it. I don't want to lose business because of this, and if the case isn't solved quickly, there's a very good chance I will. I'm visiting the people who might have known either her or Dave. You seem to be a good friend of his. I'm wondering where you were between the hours of 8:30 night before last and 8:00 yesterday morning."

There was no mistaking the look of anger that flashed across Darcy's face. "What makes you think I'd tell you that? You're not part of law enforcement. There's no reason for me to tell you."

"Well, there actually is a reason. I just came from Dave's home, and he said he spent the night with you. He told me he'd been seeing you. I think it's rather obvious that you might have benefited if Barbara died. I understand she was a very strong Catholic and wouldn't even consider a divorce. With her out of the way, you and Dave would be free to get married."

"David said he spent the night with me? Is that true?" Darcy demanded.

"Yes. Like I said, I just came from Dave's home, and he's the one who told me."

"I see. Well, if he told you that, I'll confirm that yes, he was here all night on the night in question. We both left the apartment yesterday morning about 7:00. I like to get to the high school before the teachers or students arrive, and he likes to get to his insurance agency an hour or so before his clients start arriving for scheduled appointments. We were here all night. Neither one of us left the apartment that night, so it couldn't have been either one of us who committed the crime."

"Thank you, Darcy. I'm sure you can understand how anxious I am to find out who the killer is and have this unfortunate episode behind me. It's getting very close to my busiest season, and if word gets out about this and people think there's a killer on the loose at the spa, it could be a disaster for my business."

"Yes. I understand your concerns. You seem like a nice person, and I wish I could help you, but I can't. I know nothing more than what I just told you. From what I understand, Barbara and Dave haven't been close for many years. Maybe she had a boyfriend. Those things happen, you know."

"I hadn't thought of that but maybe she did. Thanks for your help. This can't be an easy time for you. I'm sure very few people know that Dave and Barbara have had a marriage of convenience only for a long time. It must be very difficult for you to have to stay in the shadows."

"It is, but perhaps in a few months Dave and I can be seen together publicly. Maybe something good will come from something that is terribly bad. Isn't it strange where life takes you?" she said wistfully.

"Yes it is. I wish you well, Darcy. Again, thanks."

Good grief. These two must be living in la-la land if they think no one knows about their affair. And isn't it convenient that Dave and Darcy backed up each other's alibi. If one of them is the murderer, maybe they decided in advance to use each other as an alibi. Wow, that sounds real private eyeish. And Barbara having a boyfriend? No one's mentioned that. If there was any truth to it I would have thought her partner at the antique store might have mentioned it. However, with Barbara being such a strong Catholic, I have a hard time thinking of her having a romantic affair outside of her marriage. Then again, you just never know about people.

CHAPTER TWELVE

Fortunately it was one of the few nights of the year when there weren't any guests staying in the cottages, so Liz didn't have to rush home and fix appetizers and dinner for them. Knowing that no guests would be on the property, she was glad Winston would be with her. With everything that had happened in the last day and a half, she was no longer comfortable being by herself at the lodge during the night.

"Okay boy, time for dinner," Liz said as she pulled her van into the lodge's parking lot. Winston's ears went up, and as soon as she opened the door on the van, he ran up the steps to the front door of the lodge, waiting for her to open the door. A few minutes later he was hungrily eating the bowl of food Liz had put out for him. "Good grief, Winston. Ed didn't tell me you were such a big eater. I'm glad he put the amount of the dog food you're supposed to have on the instruction sheet, or I would have kept feeding you until you stopped eating! From what I'm seeing your tummy probably would have burst about that time." He wagged his tail and continued eating.

No doubt about it. This dog understands everything I'm saying!

She suddenly remembered she hadn't booked any spa treatments for Judy or herself for tomorrow. She looked at the kitchen clock and thought, *Delores should still be at the spa.*

'Hi, Delores. It's Mrs. Lucas. I want to book four spa appointments for tomorrow, two for me and two for a friend of mine, Judy Rasmussen. I'd like to book facials and massages with Cindy and Gina for both of us. I can have a massage while Judy's having a facial, and then you can reverse them. I'm open on the times. If you have to stagger us, that's fine too. Go ahead and check what's available, and I'll wait." She doodled on the pad of paper next to the phone while she waited for Delores to come back on the line.

"That's great. So you booked me for a massage at 9:00 and Judy for a massage at 10:30 and facials at 2:00 and 3:00. Perfect. See you tomorrow."

She called Judy. "Hi, hope you're still planning on coming up tomorrow, because I just booked our spa appointments."

"What time is my first appointment?" Judy asked.

"You're on for a massage at 10:30. You should be able to easily make it here by then. I have a massage at 9:00, so I'll probably be over at the spa when you get here. I reserved cottage #1 for you. We didn't have any guests today, so it should be ready for you when you get here. You can go to Bertha's office in the lodge and get the key from her. Judy, do you have a few minutes? I've got a lot to tell you."

Liz filled Judy in on everything that had happened at the spa beginning with Bertha discovering Barbara's body. She related her thinking about some of the possible suspects and finished by telling her Roger had gotten her a guard dog.

"Liz, I haven't met Roger yet, but he must really care for you if he got you a guard dog. Is this man becoming a person of interest in your life?"

"Could be, Judy, could be. I like him a lot. I really do want you to meet him. He's started coming up here quite often. In fact, he drove up last night and left early this morning. He had to get back in time for a big trial he has that started today."

"Wait a minute. The guy drove up from San Francisco the night before he's starting a big trial just to see you, and then he gets you a guard dog that's fully trained? Do you have any idea what dogs like that cost? I looked into buying one once, and we're easily talking high four figures, maybe five. That doesn't sound like a casual relationship to me. Want to tell me anything else?" she said with a teasing sound in her voice.

"Nope, nothing else to tell. Anyway, I won't be seeing him for the next few weeks because of his trial."

"If he came up the night before a big trial, I'd bet everything I own he'll be back a lot sooner than you think. For whatever it's worth, that's my two cents on the subject. When I get there tomorrow I want to hear every detail about this murder. I'm sure you've already thought of this, but it probably won't help your spa business when the word gets out."

"I'm well aware of that. The coroner told me I should try to solve the crime myself, because he doesn't think much of the abilities of the chief of police."

"You've got to be kidding! You don't know anything about private investigating, do you?"

"Well, I've never done it before, but if it means the difference between losing the spa because of bad publicity and holding on to it, I'll do everything I can to find the killer."

"I don't know if I can be of any help in catching whoever did it, but count me in. Hate for my best friend to get knocked off while she's trying to find the killer. Liz, I've got to tell you this sounds like something stranger than fiction. I'm really glad Roger got the dog for you. Maybe he had some kind of a premonition. Gotta go. Someone's at the door. See you tomorrow!"

"I don't know how this is going to work out, Winston. Judy doesn't know any more than I do about finding a killer, and it doesn't sound like the chief of police could find one if it was right in front of him. Good grief. I can't believe this is happening. Oh well, it's always better to do something rather than nothing. Roger should be home by now. I'll see if I can reach him. Anyway, I need to thank him for you."

Winston walked over to her and put his paw on her lap.

Not only does this dog know what I'm saying, he knows the right thing to do. My life is turning into something beyond bizarre. Glad Brittany and Jonah aren't around. They'd probably have me committed, and I'm not so sure they wouldn't be right.

"I'm glad you could answer your phone, Roger. Are you at home or on the road?"

"I'm home and have been for about an hour. We're still picking the jury, and when it started to get late in the day, the judge decided not to call in another panel that late in the afternoon, so he dismissed us a little early. I'm just going over some of my trial notes for tomorrow. Now, tell me about your day."

"First of all, I'm in love with Winston, and I can't thank you enough for giving him to me. He's not only beautiful, but he's the smartest dog I've ever been around. I absolutely positively believe he understands everything I say to him."

She stopped talking and held the receiver away from her ear. When he'd finally stopped laughing, she said, "Roger, you may not believe me, but just wait until you meet him, and you'll understand then. Anyway, I need to talk to you about Barbara's death. It turns out her death wasn't from natural causes or suicide, and the coroner thinks she was poisoned. Let me start from the time you left, and I'll fill you in."

She told him everything that had happened during the day beginning with Gertie and ending with her conversation with Darcy.

"Liz, I completely agree with the coroner. From what I've heard, the police chief probably couldn't find his hat if it was on his head.

Yes, you probably are going to have to do what you can to find the killer. I just want you to be careful. Do you own a gun?"

"I have one, but I haven't used it in a long time. Joe fired an employee quite a few years ago, actually before we moved here, and the employee threatened him and insinuated that I could be in danger. Joe bought a gun for me, and he took me to a pistol range several times to practice. He wanted to make sure I could use it if I ever had to. Fortunately, I never had to. Why?"

"When we get through with this call, I want you to get the gun and keep it with you. I know it's a scary thought, but a killer was on your property as recently as two nights ago. The killer may be long gone, but using poison as a way to kill someone indicates to me it was premeditated, not an emotional spur of the moment killing. If someone goes to the trouble to plan a way to get the victim to take the poison, in my mind, that person is a lot more dangerous than someone who kills someone in the heat of the moment. Do you see what I'm saying?"

"I do, and it doesn't make me feel very good. I know where the gun is, and I still have the box of ammunition Joe gave me. It's a semi-automatic pistol, and I actually got to be a pretty good shot with it, but like I said, that was a while ago."

"Trust me, Liz, it's kind of like riding a bike. Once you have the gun in your hand, you'll be good to go. Let's just hope it doesn't come to that. Keep it in your purse or on you or next to you when you're in the lodge. Is Winston scary looking or what?"

"He's big enough that I think he definitely would frighten someone. Ed gave me a sheet of paper with written instructions. One of the paragraphs lists the commands to use for protection and guarding."

"I want you to memorize those and keep him with you everywhere you go from now on. So you've talked to Darcy and Dave, and they're covering for each other."

"Yes, but I have a feeling they genuinely care about each other. I find it hard to believe that either one of them might be the killer."

"Maybe yes, maybe no. They both have a powerful motive for wanting to see Barbara dead. Very simple. If she's dead, they can be together and ride happily off into the sunset. Most crimes are committed in the name of love, heat, lust, or call it whatever you want, and for that reason it's the number one motive in murder cases. That's why homicide investigators always look to the spouse or lover first. And from what you've found out about Barbara's strong religious faith and lack of any factual basis for having a boyfriend, I wouldn't spend much time looking for a boyfriend who might have been so angry with her he would kill her. Pretty far reach, if you ask me."

"I agree. Nothing anyone has told me points in that direction and don't forget, this small town feeds on rumors. I think Gertie would have hinted at something like that if there was anything to it."

"What's your gut feeling on this guy Zack who works for you? He certainly would know the lay of the land and how to get into the cottage, probably even if the door was locked. What he said to you was odd, and remember, he did say he couldn't even tell you where he'd been."

"I think he could definitely qualify as a suspect. I guess the motive could be getting back at Dave by killing Barbara, but since everyone I've pretty much talked to knew that Dave and Darcy were having an affair, surely Zack would have known about it too. If Dave does want to marry Darcy, Zack would actually be helping Dave achieve his goal. He wants to harm Dave, not help him. It wouldn't make a lot of sense."

"Possibly," Roger said. "What about keys to the cottages? Which employees have them?"

"Bertha and I are the only two who have keys to all the cottages. I don't know if Zack does, but I wouldn't be surprised, because he's probably had to work in all of the cottages over the years. That's a good question. He may be the only one who could have entered the cottage without being allowed in by Barbara."

"That's true. So that means we have to figure out if Barbara knew the person who possibly entered her cottage. If it was Dave, she probably would have let him in. Do you know if she knew Darcy?"

"When I talked to Darcy this afternoon, she mentioned she had met Barbara only once. From everything I've heard, Barbara knew about Dave's affair with Darcy, so I can't see her inviting Darcy in, but who knows?"

"I had Sean find out everything he could about the Tiffany lamp buyer, Henry. His last name is Sanchez. He lives in a bad part of town in a run-down apartment building, but the rent is really reasonable which fits in with what you told me about his penny-pinching ways. He's well-known in the antique world and as a matter of fact, has been in most of the shops in the last week or so with a picture of the disputed Tiffany lamp, asking people if they think it's authentic. Evidently he's become totally obsessed with the notion that he was duped into buying what he now believes is a fake.

"He's not well liked and several of the terms used to describe him included 'nut case,' 'wacko,' and 'a man angry at the world.' I don't think he can be ruled out as a possible suspect. He paid a lot of money for something he's been told is a fake. Barbara had mentioned to him she was going to a local spa and even told him when she'd be returning. By process of elimination, he could deduce that it was the Red Cedar Spa. As far as knowing which cottage she was in, I suppose all one would have to do is look through the windows. He knew what she looked like. Seems to me people park their cars next to their cottage. He may have even staked her out beforehand to see what kind of a car she was driving.

"Who knows? If he's as unbalanced as people indicated to Sean, it's not that far of a stretch. What troubles me is her opening the door. Maybe she would feel safe enough in that environment to open the door without personally knowing who was standing on the other side, but I can't see her willingly letting him in."

"Please thank Sean for me. Sounds like he's a very good investigator."

"I'll thank him and yes, he's the best. He works full-time for me, and other attorneys are constantly trying to get him to work for them. He's kind of a legend in his field. He also did some work verifying the ownership of the antique shop. The woman you met with, Linda, told you the truth. The shop is in her name only. Whenever anything is bought or sold, while Barbara may have conducted the transaction, the actual purchase or sale is in Linda's name alone. Barbara's role was to obtain antiques from the people in the surrounding area and help out Linda with her knowledge about Arts and Crafts antiques and decorative items. She must have been very good because there is no record of anyone suing the shop for misrepresenting the authenticity or value of an antique and that's pretty rare."

"Oh Roger," Liz sighed, "I don't feel I'm any closer to finding out who the murderer is than I was before I talked to you. We've identified Darcy, Dave, Zack, and Henry as possible suspects, and there may be others we don't even know about. Each of them seems to have a solid alibi or explanation of why they didn't do it. It's very frustrating."

"That's true. I think I'll have Sean pay a visit to Henry tomorrow and try to find out where he was during the time frame we think she was murdered and if anyone can back it up. Oh, one thing we haven't talked about is the people who work at the spa. Have you had a chance to talk to the two women who did treatments on Barbara during the time she was at the spa?"

"No. I think I told you Judy is driving up tomorrow and staying for a couple of days. I made reservations for us with the two women who did treatments on Barbara. I figured if there's anything there, it would help if both of us saw them, and we can compare notes. Really, that's about everything."

"One other person who comes to mind is the guy who ran against Dave. What was his name?"

"Gene Harris. I don't know much about him other than he's run against Dave twice before. Why? Do you think he could have done it?"

"Yes and no. He probably hates Dave, but I go back to what we talked about with his brother. If he killed Barbara, he'd ultimately be doing Dave a favor by freeing him to marry Darcy. One of the first things people do who are running for office is find out every piece of dirt they can about their opponent. I would bet everything that Gene knew about the affair."

"Well, we're back to square one. A huge cast of characters with no one bolting into the lead at the moment. Tell you what. I had a busy day. I'm going to have a glass of wine, make some dinner, and fall into bed. I'll call you tomorrow night after our spa treatments and let you know what I found out. I have a little time between my appointments, so I think I'll go into town and talk to Bart. He's the owner of the Red Cedar Tribune, the local paper. I'd like to see what he knows. I've met him a couple of times. He's a nice guy."

"Okay, but I'm really serious about what we talked about earlier, Liz. People know you're looking into this, and that could make it very dangerous for you. Remember what I told you about keeping your gun on you and Winston next to you. Will you do that for me?"

"Yes. I promise. Good night and good luck in court tomorrow."

"Good night, sweetheart. Sweet dreams."

CHAPTER THIRTEEN

Liz felt a paw on her hand and opened her eyes to find Winston looking at her. "Need to go out, boy? You sure were quiet last night. Let me put on a robe."

One of the features she liked best about the lodge was the soundproofing. Although no guests had spent the night in the cottages last night, even if they had, she wouldn't have heard Bertha making and serving breakfast. She opened the door and let Winston out. Glancing at the clock, she saw she had about thirty minutes until her appointment for a massage at the spa.

I wonder if I should take Winston. Seems kind of silly, but I promised Roger I wouldn't go anywhere without him until this murder is solved. Better keep my promise. I'm sure Cindy will find that very strange. Oh well, it's my sandbox, and I can play in it however I want.

Liz let Winston in and fed him. She wanted him to get used to eating in her apartment rather than in the big kitchen upstairs. That way she wouldn't have to get dressed and talk to the guests until she was ready for the day. She didn't think they'd be very impressed that the owner of the lodge and spa was feeding her dog while dressed in her bathrobe and slippers.

She quickly dressed and walked upstairs to get a cup of coffee before her appointment. "Morning, Liz. I was just going over the appointment book and not only is the spa completely full today, but the cottages are all booked as well. Did you ever hear anything from the coroner about Mrs. Nelson's death?" Bertha asked.

"Yes. I've heard from the coroner. I'm sorry, I should have called you last night and told you about it." She recounted what Wes had told her.

"I saw you with the dog yesterday and wondered if you'd heard something and felt you should have a dog here for protection. Given that it was murder, I think that was the right decision."

"Actually Bertha, I wasn't planning on buying Winston. A friend of mine was adamant that I should have him for protection, and he arranged to have Winston brought to me."

"Well, however you got Winston, I think it was a good thing. This is kind of a scary place when no one's around. I wonder if this is going to affect the reservations for the spa and the cottages. Do you think it's going to be a problem for us?"

"It certainly could be. I'm going to do everything I can to see if I can discover who murdered Barbara even though I've never done anything like this before. Don't worry, we'll get through this."

"I sure hope so, because I love working here, and it seems that it's become kind of the 'in' thing for people from San Francisco. If I can help, let me know. Is it okay if I pet Winston?"

"Absolutely. Although he's a trained guard dog, he's really quite gentle, and I'd like you two to be friends."

A few minutes later Bertha said, "Time for me to get back to work, but if you ever decide you need someone to watch him for a few days, I'd love to. We've got a big back yard. Keep it in mind."

"I will and thanks, but I'm not anticipating going anywhere soon except over to the spa because it's almost time for my appointment with Cindy. Oh, I almost forgot to tell you that my friend Judy

Rasmussen will be here shortly. I told her to check in with you. Thanks, Bertha, for everything you do here."

Liz took two pork loins out of the freezer, so she could make pork medallions with a white wine sauce for dinner along with glazed carrots, rice pilaf, salad, and for dessert, the all-time favorite of her son Jonah, mud pie. Whenever he came to visit, he had a standing request for mud pie.

Good, that's out of the way, she thought. *I can get dinner ready in a few minutes, and since none of the guests have been here before, I can use the sausage cheese balls and onion bits I have in the freezer for appetizers. They won't know I served them earlier this week. After my massage, I'll come back here and make three mud pies, so they'll be ready for tonight. Easy peasy!*

"Winston, come. It's time for my spa appointment." Together they walked over to the spa with Winston stopping every ten feet to smell all the wonderful smells of his new home.

"Good morning, Delores. I want you to meet my new friend, Winston."

Winston held his paw up for Delores to shake. "Oh my gosh, Mrs. Lucas. That is the cutest trick I've ever seen. Did you teach him that?"

"No, I just got him yesterday as a present. His trainer taught him to do that when he meets people. I'm taking him into the treatment room with me. I hope Cindy isn't allergic to dogs."

"Not that I know of, but no one has ever brought a dog in here before. I know some of the guests bring their dogs and keep them in the cottages, but this is a first. Glad it's you, because I'm not sure what I would tell someone if they asked if they could bring their dog with them into the treatment room."

"Tell them it's the owner's prerogative," she said, laughing as Winston and Liz followed Delores down a short hallway to one of the massage rooms. Every time Liz was at the spa, she was glad she'd spent the extra money needed to redesign it after she and Joe bought it. She'd always loved the sound of a fountain, and one of the walls in the reception room had a stone and copper wall fountain which emitted a continuous sound of falling water. Soft music played in the background and wide pastel upholstered chairs filled the reception area. One wall was mirrored with acrylic shelves showcasing skin care and beauty products that were available for the guests to purchase.

Adjacent to the reception room was a locker room and dressing area with white fluffy towels, robes, and slippers. There were six sinks with a range of hair care and personal hygiene products displayed on acrylic trays for use by the spa patrons. All of the treatment rooms had a sound speaker for music. They were painted a soft dove gray with crisp white painted moldings and doorjambs. She'd decided not to have incense in the rooms, aware that some clients might be allergic to it. She wanted every guest to feel they were special and pampered when they left the spa, and from what she heard, they did.

Bertha was in charge of hiring the people who worked at the spa. She was diligent about checking their references and making sure their licenses were up to date. Each new spa employee was not only given written instructions on what Liz expected of them as a spa employee, they were also given an indoctrination talk by Bertha. Bertha had set the bar high, and it was one of the main reasons that the spa had become extremely popular, many of the clients coming just for spa treatments and not staying in the cottages.

"Good morning, Mrs. Lucas. I see you have a new friend. May I pet him?"

"Absolutely, Cindy. I just got him yesterday, so I want him to become familiar with the property. I hope you don't mind if he stays during the massage."

"Not at all. I love dogs. I just wish I could have one in the apartment where I live, but it really wouldn't be fair to leave a dog in it when I'm gone all day. Is there any place special you'd like me to concentrate on today?"

"No. I'd just like you to work out some of the kinks I've developed as I've gotten older. A traditional massage will be fine," Liz said.

"Okay. Why don't you turn over on your stomach, and I'll start on your shoulders and neck. As I remember, that's where you seem to store a lot of tension. Let me know if I'm hurting you."

"Will do. Is this the type of massage that most people ask for?"

"Yes. It's definitely the most popular one. Just a plain old traditional getting the kinks out type of treatment. A lot of people also like the warm stone massage. The heat loosens their muscles and seems to help in reducing tension. As a matter of fact, I was going to do one on that woman who died. She was scheduled for an appointment at 8:00 that morning. When she wasn't here at the scheduled time, I asked Delores to call Bertha, and I think that's how she was discovered."

"Yes. You're right. I only talked to her briefly at dinner. Did you and she talk much during your session?"

"Not really. She was pretty quiet. I've learned over the years that I've worked as a masseuse that there seem to be two types of clients. There are the ones who talk all the time they're on the table and want to tell me their life story because I'm a captive audience, and there are the ones who come simply to have me release the tension from their bodies so they'll feel better when they leave. I'd have to say she was in the latter category. Other than exchanging a few amenities when she first came in and thanking me when she left, I don't believe we talked at all."

"Well, I think I'll be in the latter category for the rest of the session."

An hour later, Liz thanked Cindy and told Winston to come. There were times when she wished people didn't know she was the owner. She would have preferred to have worn her robe when she came to the spa from the lodge. That's what most of the guests wore when they came from their cottages. *To heck with it*, she thought, *next time I have a spa treatment I'm going to treat myself like a guest and wear a robe.*

When they returned to the lodge she went into the kitchen, made three chocolate cookie crusts, baked them, and set them on cooling racks. Thirty minutes later, showered and dressed, she spooned toffee ice cream into them, filling the shells and put them in the freezer.

Good, that's out of the way. I can put the chocolate sauce on them later this afternoon and then whip the cream for the final layer of topping. I mean, who can resist chocolate sauce and ice cream? They'll love it!

"Winston, we're going into town. I want to talk to Bart over at the Tribune. Maybe he can shed some light on this mystery."

The Red Cedar Tribune was located in one of the oldest buildings in Red Cedar. The lumber baron who had established Red Cedar in the late 19th century had built it as an office building. Over the years, it had passed through several different owners, and now it provided a home for the local newspaper. Bart Stevenson had a reputation as an editor who presented both sides of an issue in a fair and even-handed manner, and that's why Liz was curious to speak with him about the mayor and his opponent.

"Hi," she said to the woman at the receptionist desk. "My name is Liz Lucas, and I'd like to speak with Bart Stevenson for a moment, if he's free."

"He'll probably see you," said the prim looking woman who looked like she belonged back in the 19th century with her hair tightly done up in a bun and her red and white striped blouse buttoned all the way to the top, "because it's not quite deadline time for tomorrow's paper, but he's allergic to dogs, so you might want to put that big boy back in your car."

"Of course. I'll be back in a minute. Come, Winston."

Glad she told me. Rather doubt I would have gotten much information from Bart if he was sneezing the whole time.

When she returned, Bart Stevenson was standing next to the woman's desk. "Liz, it's been a long time. Please, come back to my office." She followed him past several desks where people were feverishly working on their computers. The paper's office was in Red Cedar, but it covered the news from Portland to San Francisco and was a must read with everyone's morning coffee.

"Have a seat," he said, closing the door. "What brings you here?"

"Bart, you probably have heard that Barbara Nelson was found dead in a cottage at my spa. The coroner told me late yesterday that she didn't commit suicide, and she didn't die of natural causes. That means she was murdered. There were no physical signs of trauma on her body, so he thinks she was poisoned. I don't need to tell you what this could do to my business if it gets out. He also suggested that I look into it, because he doubted that the chief of police was capable of finding the killer. As far as people who could have a motive for seeing Barbara dead, I've come up with a few. I'd like to run them by you."

She proceeded to tell him who she had met with and what had been said by each of them. "I don't know much about Gene Harris, other than he ran against Dave in the election for mayor and was beaten by him. His brother is the handyman out at my spa. Is there anything you can tell me about him?"

He rubbed his hands together, deep in thought. "I got a phone call from someone last night who had heard Seth spouting off that Barbara was murdered, but I wanted to confirm it before I printed anything. You've just confirmed it, but I certainly understand why you'd like this to be solved ASAP. As far as Gene goes, I think he's an honorable man. Sure, he can't stand Dave, and probably for good reason. He had a political consultant see what he could find out about Dave and from what he told me, it looks like Dave may have done some things that aren't exactly considered to be aboveboard. I even wrote a couple of editorials advocating that an investigation should be undertaken to see if there was any truth to the rumors about Dave's malfeasance in office.

"One of the claims was that Dave used his influence with the county to have the highway diverted a few miles from Red Cedar to benefit some people who ran cattle on that land. After that happened a lot of maximum donations from people who either worked at the ranches, or were relatives of the owners, made their way into Dave's campaign fund. You can only give a maximum of $500 in a mayor's race.

"Gene asked my opinion as to what he should do with the information his investigator unearthed, and I told him to let it go. He simply didn't have enough evidence for me to print it or for him to put it in writing in a campaign flyer. If Gene had put his suspicions in writing in the form of a political campaign hit piece, Dave would have sued Gene for everything he had. He's not a wealthy man, and with two kids in high school he couldn't afford to risk it."

"Do you think Gene hated Dave enough to murder Barbara as a vendetta for Dave winning the election?"

"No. He hates Dave, no doubt about that, but what would he gain? Everyone knows that Darcy and Dave are seeing one another, and a lot of people know that Barbara was very active in the Catholic Church. It's not much of a stretch to assume she wasn't big on divorce, so if Gene killed her, he'd actually be doing Dave a favor by freeing him to marry Darcy. No," he said, shaking his head, "I can't see that happening."

"Well, if that's not a scenario that will work, can you think of anyone who might have a reason to murder Barbara?"

He stuck his thumbs in his red suspenders and walked over to the window. After a few moments, he turned to her and said, "You've mentioned several people you've talked to and outside of those I can't think of anyone else who may have wanted to murder Barbara. Let me ask you this. Is there anyone who would want to see the spa get a bad reputation because someone was murdered while there as a guest? Do you have any enemies? Is someone at the spa disgruntled? Have you fired anyone recently?"

Liz was quiet for several moments and then answered, "Bart, I've never even considered that possibility. I don't do the hiring. I'll have to talk to Bertha, she's the one who runs the spa, but no, I can't think of anyone. Sure, the spa is becoming popular, and I'm certain there are other spas around that may be jealous of our success, but they're far enough away that we're not competing for the same clients. I'll have to think about it."

"I wish I could help you. I'm sorry I don't have more time to spend with you, but I need to look over some articles before I okay them for tomorrow's edition. If you find out anything more or want to talk to me, give me a call. I'm not going to put anything in the paper about Barbara being murdered right now. I will have to put in tomorrow's edition that her body was found because it's common talk around town, but out of deference to you, I'll hold off for a day or so printing that she was murdered."

"Bart, I really appreciate your seeing me on no notice and not printing immediately that Barbara's death was a murder. If I find out anything, I'll let you know. Again, thanks!"

"Anytime, and for you and your spa's sake, I hope you find out who did this sooner rather than later."

She left the building and walked to her van. "Okay, Winston. Back to the spa. Judy should be finished with her treatment by now, and I need to talk to Bertha."

CHAPTER FOURTEEN

When Liz returned to the lodge, Judy was waiting for her in the great room, dressed casually in jeans and a tee-shirt, her face free of make-up and her long black hair casually caught up in scrunchy. Tall and graceful, and even though she was in her early 50's, she'd never lost the ability to turn everyone's head whenever she entered a room. She and Judy met when their children were in preschool together. They'd remained close friends for all of the years in between.

When Judy was a young woman, she came to California lured by the film industry. In the small rural Kansas town where she grew up, she was the acknowledged beauty, but in California she was just one more beauty. Liz remembered Judy telling her about the moment she knew with certainty she'd never make it big in the movies. She was sitting in a movie director's reception area getting ready to read for a part in a movie. Judy told her she'd looked around the room at the other women who were there to read for the part, and realized every woman in the room was just as beautiful as she was. She couldn't handle another rejection and walked out. A few months later she married a movie producer and gave up any thoughts of trying to become a star. The marriage lasted only seven years, but Judy walked away from it with a large financial settlement.

She'd met an internet mogul from San Francisco a short time later, moved there, and married him. The marriage lasted ten years, and once again Judy managed to leave the marriage with a large divorce settlement. It probably hadn't hurt that she'd caught husband number two in bed with their housekeeper. When she opened the bedroom door and found them in a compromising position, a light bulb went off in her head, and she knew her husband had fathered the housekeeper's son. Something about the little boy's appearance had always bothered her. Her husband and the little boy shared a striking resemblance to one another. She'd angrily confronted him, and he hadn't denied it. A few days later he instructed his attorney to make sure the divorce settlement to her was generous. It may have been guilt money, but Judy felt he owed it to her. Since then there had been a number of men in her life, but not one special man. She had vowed to Liz that two marriages were enough. She made a promise to herself she would never marry again.

Liz walked over to where Judy was sitting looking out at the ocean. "Hey, lady, glad you could come up. How was your massage?" she said, giving Judy a big hug.

"It was great, but is this the guy Roger gave you? You didn't tell me he was this big. I don't think I'd ever worry about my safety if he was protecting me."

"I don't, now that I have him." Liz turned to Winston, "Winston, I want you to meet Judy. Judy, this is Winston."

Winston walked over to Judy, sat down next to her, and extended his paw as if to shake her hand.

"Are you kidding me? This is about the cutest thing I've ever seen. Does he do other tricks?" she asked, shaking his paw.

"He does, but I haven't had time to go over them. Remember, I only got him yesterday, and my mind has been on a few other things."

"I understand, and I want you to tell me everything, but first I have a question. Why did you name this place the Red Cedar Spa? I mean, I know there are a lot of red cedars in the area, but there are also a lot of other kinds of trees, why red cedar?"

"If you remember, after you and I first came here I went back to San Francisco and convinced Joe we needed to buy it. It was named 'Spa By The Ocean' at the time, and I kind of wanted a better name, something a little more descriptive. Anyway, I thought the forests around here were pretty spectacular, so I searched the Internet to find out what I could about them. I ran across the legend of the red cedar. It's a Native American legend which describes the origins of the Western Red Cedar. According to what I found out, the legend talked about a generous older man who gave the people whatever they needed. When he died, the Great Spirit said a red cedar tree would grow and multiply where he was buried, and it would give the people what they needed, just as he had done. The trees would provide roots for baskets, bark for clothing, and wood for shelter. I've placed a piece of parchment paper in each of the cottages with the words of the legend written on it, and it concludes by saying 'We hope the Red Cedar Spa will give you what you need.'"

"I'm impressed, Liz. Who would have thought that anyone who can cook like you do could also be so good at marketing? Nice job!"

"Thanks. Now that I'm looking at the potential for a lot of bad publicity, maybe it will help us keep the doors open. Anyway, I'm starving, and I'll bet you are too. I'll make some lunch for us, and I'll tell you everything I've learned about the murder and the possible suspects."

"I'd appreciate it, because I'm dying of curiosity, and I'm pretty hungry too. What are you offering?"

"Thought I'd fix a crab Louie salad. I haven't had one in a while and it's not something I serve at dinner. I've also got some sourdough bread that I'll heat up, and that should be plenty."

An hour later Judy sat back and said, "You've definitely had a few full days. I may have to move here just to make sure you're not getting into any trouble. Seems like you have your hands full at the moment. Would you mind if I lived here permanently? You could cook all this fabulous food, and I could just sit and look at the ocean and pretend I know something about solving crimes, but I do love it here. What's next on today's agenda?"

"You know you're always welcome here. As far as this afternoon's agenda. I have a facial at 2:00, and you have one at 3:30. I took the earlier one so I could be back in plenty of time to get tonight's dinner ready. We have a full house."

"I'll help. Just tell me what to do."

"Thanks. I meant to ask you what you thought of your massage therapist this morning. She was the therapist who gave Barbara, the woman who was murdered, a massage the day she died."

"I like her. I'm not real big on talking when I'm being worked on, but she gave a great massage and couldn't have been nicer. I really don't have much of anything to say about her."

"Okay. I'd also like your opinion on the woman who's going to be giving you your facial this afternoon. She gave a facial to Barbara the day she died."

"Will do. Anything else I need to know or do?"

"Not that I can think of. Why don't you go back to your cottage and relax until your facial, or feel free to stay here and look at the ocean. I need to talk to Bertha before I have my facial, and I don't have much time. I promised Roger I'd take Winston with me everywhere I go for the time being, so he'll be coming with me when I have my facial."

"Like I said when I talked to you on the phone, any guy who gives a woman an expensive present like that is pretty serious about her."

"Come on, Judy. He gave me a dog. It's no big deal."

"Yeah. Well, believe me, he spent as much on that dog as he would have spent on a very expensive diamond bracelet, and if he'd given you expensive jewelry I don't think you'd be saying, 'Come on, Judy' in that tone of voice, would you?"

"Hadn't thought about it that way. No I probably wouldn't."

"I think I've made my point," she said walking over to the door. "What time is dinner?"

"Wine and appetizers are at 6:30. Dinner is served at 7:15. Why don't you come around 6:00 or so, and we'll have a chance to compare facials."

"Consider it done. See you then. Bye, Winston."

Winston gave a short bark at being acknowledged and raised one of his paws.

You have got to be kidding me. If the spa goes south, just might put him in the circus.

CHAPTER FIFTEEN

Liz knocked on the door marked "Manager" and entered the large office that overlooked the ocean. "Bertha, do you have a minute? I need to talk to you."

"Of course. You sound like you're serious, what is it?"

Liz told her about the conversation she'd had with Bart regarding the possibility that the spa was being targeted in connection with Barbara's death. "You're the one who does all the hiring and firing. Have you fired anyone recently or have there been any disgruntled employees that you can think of?"

Bertha was quiet for a few moments, deep in thought. "Liz, I can't think of anyone who has been unhappy. There seems to be a genuine camaraderie among the employees at the spa and, believe it or not, I can't remember ever having to fire anyone. You pay well, and the employees seem to love working here. Just to give you an example of the tight knit group we have, I just hired a facialist by the name of Gina. I think you briefly met her the other morning. She was the one who gave Barbara her facial prior to her death. Anyway, the day I hired her she was talking to a couple of the employees at the spa about finding a place to live, and two of them offered to let her share the cabin they were renting."

"I thought that's pretty much what you'd say. I was sure if there had been a problem, you would have alerted me to it. That's interesting about Gina. I'm having a facial in a few minutes from her. I didn't realize she was that new."

"She is, and I've gotten very good feedback on her. I called the spa she'd been working at previously, and they gave her a glowing referral. They were sorry she'd left, but knew she was ready to move on to a bigger spa."

"Well, I guess that's a dead end. If you think of anything else, let me know." She turned and was walking towards the door when Bertha called her back.

"Liz, there is something I meant to tell you. I'm sure it's nothing, and with everything that's happened over the last couple of days, it slipped my mind. I'm sorry."

"I can certainly understand something slipping your mind. What is it?"

"When I came to work the morning I found Barbara, I noticed that the security lights weren't working. They come on at 6:00 p.m. this time of year and stay on throughout the night and don't go off until it's fully light. I think this time of year they're on until 7:00. That particular morning I came to the lodge a little early, because I had to take Hank to work since his car was in the shop. You know he works as the manager of the supermarket in town, and he wanted to be there about 6:30, so I probably got here about 6:40. Anyway, I noticed the security light we have as you turn off the highway onto the lane wasn't on. Then when I drove up to the lodge parking lot, I noticed the spa and lodge security lights weren't on either. I thought maybe a circuit breaker had blown. When Zack came back to work yesterday, the first thing I had him do was check on it, and sure enough, he had to trip one of the circuit breakers to restore the lights, and they're working fine now. I don't know how this fits in with anything, but as I said, I meant to tell you, but it slipped my mind."

"Thanks, Bertha, now that you mention it, I do remember they weren't on yesterday morning when a friend of mine left early.

Interesting. It is strange, but I don't see how it would play a part in Barbara's death. I better go now, or I'm definitely going to be late for my appointment. See you later. Come on, Winston."

*****

Delores reached down and scratched behind Winston's ears and then stood up and escorted Liz to a room identical to the massage room she'd been in earlier and told her to lie down on the treatment bed, face up. There was a knock on the door and a young woman said, "Hello, Mrs. Lucas. It's Gina, we met the other day."

"It's good to see you again. I hope you don't mind that I brought my dog with me. I just got him yesterday, and I'm trying to acclimate him to his new surroundings."

"No, that's fine with me." She knelt down and put her hand out to pet Winston. As she did so, they both heard a low growl coming from him.

"Winston, no. I'm sorry, Gina. As I said, I just got him yesterday, and something must have spooked him." She looked down at Winston who was as close to her as he could be without getting up on the table with her. "Easy boy, easy."

"Don't worry about it, Mrs. Lucas. Some people have a way with dogs. I don't. They never seem to like me. It's okay, I'm used to it. I need to ask you if you have any skin conditions I should be aware of."

"No. My skin has never been a problem. I've had a few facials, but none recently."

Gina mixed a compound and placed a soft mask over Liz's eyes, examining her skin with the help of the light from a strong lamp. Liz felt Gina's hands gently moving over her face.

"Your skin's in very good condition. What I like to do with someone in your age group is a peel. It seems to work well. You may experience a little pinkness afterwards as well as a tingling sensation, but those will go away in a couple of days. Is it all right with you if I do that kind of a procedure?"

"Yes, that's fine. I understand you're living with two of the other women who work at the spa. How did you happen to come here? This spa is a little off the beaten track."

"I like it here," Gina said, stroking Liz's face with soft pads soaked in a cleanser, "I live nearby in a small cabin with Stephanie and Nikki. I got my aesthetician's license in Seattle and planned on practicing there, but my mother and I had a disagreement. Actually, I surprised her with a visit one weekend and found her in bed with my boyfriend, Scott, so I packed up and left the state. I really feel fortunate to work here. Among spa employees, you have the reputation as being the most selective about who you hire."

"Thanks, but how horrible for you! Your mother and your boyfriend? How long ago was that?"

"Over two years ago, but my mother called me last night," she said with a catch in her voice, "to tell me she and Scott had gotten married. I'm still a little shaken up by it, and I have no idea how she got my cell phone number. Maybe she got it from Scott. I know the only reason she married him was to hurt me. She's hated me ever since I can remember. My father left her when I was very young, and she always told me I reminded her of him, because I looked so much like him." Her hand shook slightly as she applied gel to Liz's face.

"Gina, I can't imagine how painful that must have been. Do you have brothers or sisters?"

"No. I'm an only child. I don't know what happened to my father. My mother and I were never close. Please don't talk anymore because I need this gel to set. I'm going to put a heat lamp on you to dry it out a little faster. I'm also going to put some mitts on your hands and wrists. They have a warm moisturizer in them. Just relax. I'll be back in a few minutes."

Liz's face was tingling, and she was very aware of heat coming from the lamp. She wanted to scratch her face, but figured that probably wasn't a good idea. Plus, her hands were covered with the mitts. Her thoughts turned to Gina.

How hard it must be for her. I can't imagine a mother doing that to her child. Sounds like she had a miserable childhood. Who wouldn't be upset by a phone call like that? I can understand why her hand was shaking when she applied the gel to my face. Liz drifted off for a few minutes and was awakened by a knock on the door and seconds later, the sound of the door opening.

"It's Gina, Mrs. Lucas. How are you doing?"

"I'm fine, but my face feels itchy."

"That's perfectly normal. I'll take off the gel and apply a soothing aloe product on it that will counter the effects from the peel. Your skin will soon feel like a newborn's." She gently removed the gel and applied the aloe based lotion. "I'll be back shortly. Again, just relax."

Whew, that feels a lot better, Liz thought. *I can't wait to see what my complexion looks like.*

Gina returned in a few minutes, removed the aloe lotion from Liz's face, and the mitts from her hands. "I'm applying a moisturizer to your face. I like to close these sessions by massaging the neck and shoulders. Will that be all right?"

"Yes, go ahead."

"All right, Mrs. Lucas, I'm finished," she said a few minutes later." I think you'll be very happy with how you look. As I said earlier, you might be a little pink, and your face may feel a little prickly, but it should be gone by tomorrow."

"Gina, I wish you well. I'm sorry for what you've gone through, but don't judge all people by what your mother and Scott have done to you. There are a lot of really good people out there. Think about trying to find one of them, and I'm sure your life will be much better."

When she got back to her apartment and went into the bathroom to take a shower, she noticed how pink her face was, but decided it was a healthy look.

I don't think I'll need any makeup tonight other than a little mascara and lipstick.

CHAPTER SIXTEEN

The appetizers were in the oven, the wine was uncorked, and the candles had been lit. The only things missing were Judy and the guests. Liz went downstairs, fed Winston, and came back upstairs just as Judy walked through the front door.

"You look great," Liz said. "Maybe a little pink, but Gina said I'd probably be that way for a day or so, so I guess you will be too."

"I'm fine with the pink, just wish this itching would go away. I used a lot of the spa moisturizer you provided in the cottage. Maybe that will help. Do you have any aloe vera?"

"No, I've been meaning to tell Zack to plant some, but I keep forgetting. I need to do that. When we lived in San Francisco I had some right next to the back door, and I can't tell you how many times I cut that plant and used it when I'd burn my hand on something I was cooking or the kids got sunburned. If we're still itching tomorrow, I'll go to the drug store in town and get some aloe vera gel. So what did you think of Gina?" she asked, handing Judy a glass of wine.

"I thought she was very good. My complexion looks like a newborn's. She's nice, but since you're asking, I'll be honest with you. I thought there was something a little off with her. It's nothing I can put my finger on, just a sense."

"I think I know why." Liz told Judy about the conversation she'd had with Gina regarding her mother and Scott. She concluded by saying, "If that had happened to me and my mother had called me and told me that my boyfriend and she had gotten married, I'd probably be a little off, too."

"I agree, and it certainly could be the reason I felt that way. Now, what can I do to help you tonight? I need to pay you back for the all this kind hospitality."

"Just be your normal charming self and entertain everyone while I put the finishing touches on the meal. Everything's ready to go, so it should be easy peasy."

"No problem. That's what I'm best at."

*****

Liz closed the door after the last guest left and Judy was putting the last of the dishes in the dishwasher. "Judy, I need to let Winston out. It's been awhile and I sure don't want him to have an accident on this nice wooden floor. Winston, outside."

When she and Winston returned, Judy said, "You mentioned the trainer who brought Winston to you also gave you a sheet of instructions. I'm curious what else he's trained to do besides shake hands and act like a human being."

"I've got it downstairs. Be right back."

Liz handed Judy the sheet of paper that Ed had given her. Judy spent a few minutes looking at it and said, "I can't believe any dog can do these things. That man must have spent hours working with him. I don't want to try any of the things he can do since he's your dog, but did you notice the warning signs he wrote, things that you should take note of if they happen?"

"No, as I told you, I haven't had time to read it thoroughly. Why, did you find something interesting?"

"Well, let's put it this way. I'm just glad he didn't growl at me when he met me."

"What are you talking about?"

"It says here that if Winston growls when he's introduced to someone, you should be on alert. He's been trained to warn you if there's danger, particularly when it's a social situation rather than a situation where physical force is necessary. Like I said, glad I wasn't the target of a growl." She looked over at Liz, who seemed to be deep in thought. "What are you thinking about?"

Liz was chewing on her lower lip, a habit Judy remembered meant she was concerned about something. "Judy, when I introduced Gina to Winston, Gina bent down to put her hand on Winston, and he growled. It was the first time I'd heard him growl. I was surprised and gave him a command to be quiet. Gina pulled back, saying that dogs generally didn't like her. I can't figure out what that was all about."

"I told you I thought something was off with her. Maybe Winston agrees with me. Keep it in mind because this Ed guy was very clear when he wrote that you should take notice if Winston growls in a social situation."

"I don't know where to go with this, but I just remembered something else. I was lying on the table in the room when Gina walked in. Winston immediately came over and stood next to me. Actually I think if I'd asked him to, he would have jumped up on the table to be close to me. It was almost as if he was protecting me, but from what? Gina?"

"I have no idea. I'm just telling you what it says on the instruction sheet Ed gave you. Anyway, I've had a long day. I had to get up early to make sure I wouldn't get caught in traffic and miss my massage. I'm taking my itchy face and heading back to my cottage. See you in the morning. Have any plans for us tomorrow or are we just going to sit and watch the ocean all day?"

"No major plans. I'm going to call Roger after you leave and see what he found out about the Tiffany lamp guy. Other than that, I'm not sure what else I can do to try and find out who killed Barbara. I suppose I could talk to the possible suspects again, but I have a feeling I'm missing something. I've always had something I like to call a niggle. It's like an inner voice telling me something. Obviously I can't turn it on or off or control it, because if I could I wouldn't have this feeling that I'm missing something. Maybe it will come to me during a dream tonight," she said laughing as she opened the door for Judy. She turned to Winston, "Say good night to Judy."

"Woof," he barked to Judy as she walked out the door grinning. "Love that dog," she said to Liz over her shoulder. "Might just have to contact that guy about getting his brother or sister for me."

*****

"Hi Liz, I'm glad you called. I tried calling you earlier, but you must not have had your cell phone on you. How is everything?" Roger asked.

"Before we talk about what's going on in my life, I want to hear about your trial. What's happening? Did you finish selecting the jury?"

"Yes. The prosecuting attorney will start presenting his case tomorrow. From what I've seen, I think it will take several days, and then I'll be on with my witnesses. My two week estimate is going to be pretty close. Now tell me about your day."

She spent the next few minutes filling him in on her meeting with Bart, her conversation with Bertha, her spa treatments, and Judy's remarks about Winston. She ended by asking, "Was Sean able to find out anything about Henry Sanchez's whereabouts on the night Barbara was murdered?"

"Yes, evidently our boy is a bit of a drinker and frequents a neighborhood bar near his home. Sean found out he was in the bar early on the evening of the murder but left about ten saying he had to go to a meeting. No one at the bar thought much about it because he's such a strange bird, but without actually having him arrested and having to provide an alibi, I don't think there's much more we can do with him right now. However, I definitely still consider him a possible suspect."

"From everything I've heard about him, he does seem sort of weird. Maybe he was meeting someone about some antique they wanted to sell him."

"Could be. Liz, I want to talk to you some more about what Bart said. Can you think of anyone who would want to see the spa fail or who would want to harm you?"

"No. When Bart said that, I was really surprised. I can't think of anyone I would consider as an enemy, and as for the spa, like I said earlier, I'm sure there are people who are jealous of our success, but we're not really in competition with any other spa. There's no other facility like ours for miles around, probably the closest one would be in San Francisco. That just doesn't make sense."

"All right. Let's look at this from a different angle. Who would know how to trip the circuit breaker for the security lights? Zack, of course, but is there anyone else? Would any of the employees even know where the circuit breaker is located?"

"I don't know, and I don't think Bertha knows much about things like that, plus she's the most loyal employee I have. As for the other spa employees, why would they? I've been told I pay better than any of the other spa owners, and they all seem to sincerely like working here. If something happened to the spa, they'd lose their jobs, so it's certainly in their best interests to keep it going."

"I agree with everything you're saying, but two things concern me. First of all tripping the circuit breaker to the security lights. Evidently that was done the night Barbara was murdered. That's a very odd coincidence, and I don't believe in coincidences. If someone didn't want to be seen entering Barbara's cottage, what better way than to get rid of the security lights?"

"The only person I can think of who would know how to do that is Zack, and we've already talked about how having Barbara dead would help Dave, and we agreed that Zack wouldn't knowingly do anything to help him. I'm at a complete loss. What's number two?"

"This thing with Winston. If Winston felt that Gina was a threat to you, I have to believe she is. I know that's hard for you to believe, but knowing how thoroughly Ed trains his dogs, I think you need to find out more about her. Actually, I'm going to call Ed in the morning and tell him what happened. He might have some insight into it. I've got to do a little more trial preparation for tomorrow, so I'm going to have to sign off. Remember, I want you to keep your gun and Winston with you. Promise?"

"Yes, I promise, although it's probably not too necessary tonight, because the cottages are full."

"I'm glad to hear that, but since nothing is making a lot of sense right now, I'm not going to rely on a full house to keep you safe. Sleep well."

"You too, and Roger, thanks for all your help and concern."

"If I haven't said it before, I'll say it now. I really care about you, and I'm really concerned about this situation. Be safe."

CHAPTER SEVENTEEN

It was a long, miserable night for Liz. Sleep eluded her as the fiery heat and itching on her face became more and more unbearable. She got up several times in the middle of the night to apply a moisturizer. Each time she looked in the mirror, her face seemed to be redder and getting bigger.

Gina said I might have some redness, but this is ridiculous. I wonder how Judy's doing.

In the morning, she waited until the guests had finished breakfast and then went upstairs to get some coffee. It was still too early to go over to Judy's cottage or to the drug store. She got dressed and waited as the minutes slowly ticked by.

At 9:00, Bertha walked into the kitchen where Liz was reading the morning paper for the third time.

"Liz, are you all right? Your face is really red!"

"If it's any consolation, it feels as hot as it looks. I'm just waiting for the drug store to open, so I can go into town and get some aloe vera."

"I wish you'd said something earlier. I have a tube of it in my desk. My hands bother me from to time, and it really seems to help, but before I get it, I need to talk to you."

"Of course. What is it? You look worried."

"I am. I just got a call from Delores over at the spa, and we might have a problem. Gina didn't show up for work today, however her two roommates are at the spa, and the three of them always ride to work together. Delores asked them where Gina was, and they said they didn't know, that she'd never come home last night. The problem is the spa is almost fully booked today. I have a friend who's a retired facialist. I just called her and asked her if she could fill in for the day, and she said she'd be here in a few minutes, so I can cover today's appointments, but I'm concerned about Gina. I thought you and I should talk to her roommates and see if we can find out anything from them. They'll be here in a few minutes. They each have a little time to spare before their next appointments."

"Thanks, Bertha. When I had my treatment from Gina yesterday she didn't mention anything to me about not being able to come to work today. I don't know what it could be."

"I don't either. Maybe I'm just spooked from Barbara's death and the mystery of the security lights not being on, but I thought we should find out what we can. I'll go get the aloe vera."

She returned a few minutes later and handed it to Liz.

"Thanks," she said, slathering the aloe vera on her face. "Oh, that feels so much better. Mind if I keep it until I can get some of my own?"

"Of course not. I don't need it."

*****

The two massage therapists, Nikki and Stephanie, walked into the kitchen looking concerned. Before either Liz or Bertha could say a word Nikki asked, "Mrs. Lucas, what in the world has happened to your face?"

"Nikki, I have no idea. Gina said it would be a little pink and itchy, but this seems way beyond to me."

"I've never seen anyone's face look like that after a treatment."

"I'm sure it will be fine, but that's not why we asked you here," Liz said. "Bertha and I are worried about Gina. You mentioned to Bertha that she didn't come home last night. Is there anything you can tell me about her? Is that unusual?"

Nikki and Stephanie exchanged glances, and Liz could see they appeared to be reluctant to say anything about Gina. "Please, if Gina's in trouble, I'd like to know. Bertha mentioned to me that she's only been here for a week. Did either one of you know her before? What made you decide to ask her to share your cabin?"

Stephanie took a deep breath and began to speak. "No. We didn't know her. When she was hired, she said she was going to have to find a place to live, and she asked me if I knew of anyone who needed a roommate. Nikki and I had talked about getting someone else to share the rent, and it seemed very natural to ask her to join us, so we did, and she moved in with us. Privately, after the first day or so, we wondered if we'd made the right decision. She seemed a little odd. It was nothing we could put our fingers on, but something didn't seem to be quite right with her."

"Did anything happen this week to reinforce that feeling?"

Once again they looked at each other and then Nikki began to speak. "Yes. She'd mentioned she was estranged from her mother. She actually said she hated her. A couple of days ago she mentioned that one of her clients looked exactly like her mother. I remember her laughing and saying her mother would get what was coming to her someday soon. I didn't know what she meant by that, but I thought it was kind of strange."

"I agree. I think that's very weird. I wonder what she did mean," Liz said. "Gina told me her mother had called night before last and told her that she and Gina's old boyfriend had gotten married. Gina seemed quite shaken by it. Were either one of you there when she got the call?"

"We both were," Stephanie said. "She was pretty hysterical after the call. I remember she threw her phone down on the floor and started crying and screaming. She kept saying how much she hated her mother. I think I said something about how her mother couldn't hurt her because she lived so far away. I also told her she was the best facialist at the spa and how happy her clients were with their treatments. We tried to calm her down without much success. Finally she went into her bedroom and collapsed on her bed."

Nikki interrupted her. "What really scared us, Mrs. Lucas, is that it was kind of like something inside of her just snapped. It's as if whatever we'd sensed before had come undone. We heard her crying all night and saying over and over she wished her mother was dead. Steph and I even talked about suggesting she get some help, you know, like from a shrink."

"Good grief. On one hand I feel very sorry for her, but on the other hand I really do find this frightening. How was she yesterday morning? I know she came to work yesterday, because she gave me a facial."

"She seemed much better. I woke her up and took some toast and jam to her. She said she'd be ready to go to work in fifteen minutes, and she was. Actually, she seemed like a totally different person from the night before. I thought maybe she'd decided to accept the situation and move on. Now I don't know."

"What do you mean?" Bertha asked.

"We always met by the front door when the spa closed. The two of us waited for her for about twenty minutes yesterday after the spa closed. We thought it was kind of odd that she was late because she liked to get back to our cabin before it got dark. She's really into herbs and plants and she liked to go out in the forest as soon as we got home and look for things. She usually returned when it got dark with a big sack full of stuff. I don't know anything about them, but she seemed to be pretty knowledgeable. She said she sometimes used them in homemade formulas she made for her clients. There was no sign of her, so we left and went back to our cabin. She never came home last night."

"Weren't you concerned about that?" Liz asked.

"Not really. It's not unusual for the employees to go into town to Eddie's Place and have a few beers. Once in a while there's an attraction between one of them and one of the guys in there, and they get together for the night."

I'm not going to say anything about that kind of social activity. I'll just come off looking like some old woman completely out of touch with current times and how the younger generation acts these days.

Liz looked at the kitchen clock. "You two need to get back to work pretty soon. Is there anything else you want to tell me? Do you know where Gina's mother lives?"

"Yes," Nikki answered. "One time Gina mentioned that she'd grown up in Bellingham, Washington. I think she said her mother still lived there and now so did Scott."

"Thank you both. If you think of anything else, please let Bertha or me know."

When they were gone, Liz turned to Bertha and said, "What do you think?"

"I don't know. I'm going to post a job opening on our web site, because I have a feeling she isn't coming back. I don't know where she went or why, but even if she returned, I wouldn't want her back. That kind of behavior is totally unprofessional, and if I ignored it, it would set a bad precedent for the rest of the staff."

"I agree. As always, thanks."

Bertha reached down and patted Winston. "Love this dog, Liz.

He's a keeper." Winston responded to the attention he was getting by sitting up and lifting up his paw, as if to say, "Thank you for saying such nice things about me."

"Couldn't agree more. I'm off to see how Judy's doing this morning and then into town to get some aloe vera. Winston, come."

When Judy answered Liz's knock on her door and opened it, the two of them spent a moment simply staring at each other in shock. The extreme redness and the swelling on their faces were identical.

"Quick. Come inside," Judy said. "I don't think either one of us should go out in public looking like this. I know Gina said I might be pink, but this isn't pink. I'm verging on a dark red plum color, and as swollen as my face is, I probably look like one."

"I brought you some aloe vera. It really helps the itching. I've had to keep my hands by my sides trying to control the urge to claw at my face. I wonder if something was wrong with whatever Gina put on us."

"Don't know. I was just getting ready to go over to the spa and ask her."

"Unfortunately, you're not going to be able to do that. Actually, there's a little excitement going on at the spa at the moment." She filled Judy in on her conversation with Nikki and Stephanie.

"Swell. Now we don't even know what we can use to get rid of this. I'm going to call my daughter. She has a good friend who's a facialist. Maybe she can find something out. I'll come over to the lodge and tell you what she says after I talk to her and take a shower. Thanks for the aloe. We definitely need to get some more of this. I wonder if the spa sells it. If they do, we could avoid going into town and frightening people."

"Good thought. I'll call Delores and if they do, I'll have someone from the spa bring it to us. See you later."

*****

Liz returned to the lodge and dialed Roger's number. She knew he'd want to know what was happening concerning her investigation into Barbara's death. She fully expected to leave a message, certain court was already in session.

"Good morning Liz. How are you today?"

"Actually, I was ready to leave a voice mail. I thought you'd be in the courtroom doing your thing. I'll just be a minute as I'm sure your time is limited. I think it's a good thing you can't come up for a week or so. I'm having a terrible reaction to the facial I had yesterday, and believe me, it's made me look absolutely horrible, not to mention the extreme pain and burning sensation I'm having. Judy's having the exact same reaction. I don't think you'd even recognize me. My face is terribly swollen and red. As if that wasn't enough, we're having a bit of a crisis at the spa."

She told Roger about the conversation she'd had with Nikki and Stephanie.

He was quiet for a minute. "I have a dermatologist I use occasionally as an expert witness in court. Let me give him a call and see what he says. I'm in the hallway outside the courtroom, and I don't know if I can get through to him before court starts, but if not, I'll get back to you as soon as I can. And about this Gina woman. She sounds deranged. I'm glad she's not there. You don't need someone like her working in the spa. Bertha is absolutely right about getting someone else to replace her. Uh-oh, gotta go. Looks like we're going to start and don't want to irritate the judge this early in the trial. Talk to you later."

CHAPTER EIGHTEEN

Darlene had just left the lodge after delivering two bottles of aloe vera from the spa when Liz's cell phone rang. She looked at the screen and saw it was Roger.

"Liz, I only have a moment, so I'll be brief. I got in touch with the dermatologist I told you about earlier this morning. He said, based on what I told him, it sounds like you definitely are having a reaction to something contained in the gel that Gina applied to you when you had your facial. He told me you or the spa manager need to look at everything that's in Gina's treatment room cabinets. Call me back with a list of all the products, and if I don't answer, leave a voice mail with the list of what you find in them. The doctor said it's critical to do it immediately because you may need an antidote."

"I'll take care of it right now. Thanks."

"Gotta go."

She called Darlene and asked, "Is Gina's treatment room being used by anyone?" She listened for a moment. "Good. I'm glad you thought to put Bertha's friend in one of the other rooms. I'll be coming in the back door in a couple of minutes and making a list of the different products she has stored in her cabinets. When I'm finished, I'll leave by the back door, so don't be concerned if you see lights on in her room or you hear some sounds. It will just be me. I won't be long. Thanks."

She walked over to the spa with Winston and entered through the back door. She took all of the jars and bottles out of the cabinets in Gina's treatment room and began to make a list of them. When she was finished she returned them to the cabinets and left with the list of the products Gina used when she gave a facial to a client.

As soon as she got back to the lodge, she called Roger and left a voicemail message for him. "Roger, I'm sure you're in trial. Here's the list your doctor friend wanted. I don't know a thing about any of them. I'll have my cell phone with me if you want to get in touch with me. Please tell your friend thanks." She then read the names off of the list she'd made when she inventoried the products Gina had stored in her treatment room cabinets.

When she was finished, she turned to Winston and said, "Winston, let's go see Judy and see if she's found out anything."

"Come in," Judy said when Liz knocked on her cottage door. "I just got off the phone with Tiffany, and I'm really getting concerned. I told her everything that had happened and how worried we were about what was happening to our faces. She told me she'd call her friend and get her opinion. I was just about to go to the lodge and get you because her friend said I need to get a list of everything that Gina used when giving a client a facial."

"I'm ahead of you. Roger called a dermatologist he uses as an expert witness, and he said the same thing. I've already called Roger back and left a message on his phone with a list of the products Gina used. Here they are," she said, handing the list to Judy.

"I have more to tell you," Judy said, "but let me call her friend directly with this list and see what she says. She put on her reading glasses and punched numbers into her phone. "Hi, Lisa. Here's the list of the products that were in the facialist's storage cabinets." She began reading them off. Liz could hear a scream at the other end of the line and Judy resumed talking. "Yes, I said phenol. It's spelled p-h-e-n-o-l. Why? Is that not a good thing?" She was quiet for a moment, her eyes widening. "Lisa, are you sure?" She listened again. "Well, what can we do?"

A few minutes later she thanked Lisa, ended the call, and turned to Liz. "She said that phenol is also known as carbolic acid. Evidently it's an extremely caustic substance, and it can cause severe blistering when applied to human skin. She said no aesthetician would ever use it on someone's skin without the client's knowledge and consent because it's so dangerous and would very likely cause the exact reactions we're having. She said to keep applying water on it, and that should help. She also said since we didn't take it into our systems we should be okay and to use the aloe vera. It will probably take a couple of weeks for the redness and the swelling to completely disappear. Good grief, Liz, I'm having a hard time believing it was a mistake, since it happened to both of us."

"I'm not quite there. I wonder if she inadvertently grabbed the phenol instead of something else. We may never know. What else did you want to tell me?"

"You know my daughter Tiffany is a psychologist, and she has a theory about all of this. I think it may be a very good theory, but I don't know what to do about it."

"You're talking in riddles. What did she say?"

"Tiffany wonders if Gina deliberately prepared a gel that would cause the adverse reactions we're having. Her thinking is that Gina hates her mother, and because we're in the same age group as her mother, we became stand-ins for her mother."

"That makes her sound even more unbalanced and dangerous."

"Well, that might be true, but let's get back to Tiffany's theory. If it's true, talk about being in the wrong place at the wrong time! It reminds me of the time when I was in college walking back to my dorm after I'd been studying in the library one night. Some guy had taken his date home from a fraternity party after drinking too much beer and drove his car onto the sidewalk where I was walking.

Fortunately, the car just tapped me, but it was enough to cause some huge bruises on my leg. That's what I mean about being in the wrong place at the wrong time. Maybe that's what happened to us at the spa."

"Judy, if she really is unbalanced and has mentally snapped, and since she mentioned several times she'd like to see her mother dead, I wonder if she's going to Washington to try and kill her mother. I know it sounds pretty far-fetched, but the situation that seems to be developing may be a lot more dangerous than putting some acid solution on our faces. What do you think?"

Judy was quiet for a few moments. "I think you're absolutely right. We probably should call the police department in the town where her mother lives and alert them of our suspicions. Maybe they can keep her mother's house under surveillance and see if Gina shows up."

"You've been watching too many crime shows on television," Liz said. "Do you really think if we call the police department because of a suspicion we have, based on no firm facts, I might add, that they will assign one or two policemen to see if she shows up? Sorry, but I don't see that happening. They'll probably take the information down, and as soon as the phone call is completed, dismiss the whole thing as just another nut case call like they probably get every day. I know that's what I'd think if I were them."

Liz began to feel a slight niggle in the back of her mind, that inner sense that only seemed to make itself known when it needed to really get her attention.

"What is it, Liz? You've got a really funny look on your face."

"Judy, I have no idea where this is coming from, but I have the strongest feeling that Gina is planning to kill her mother, and I have to stop her."

"Are you kidding? What can you do from here? You didn't like my idea of calling the police."

"I have to do this. It's my spa, and it's already getting a black eye from Barbara's death. All I need is for a spa employee to commit murder. I'm going to Washington, to Bellingham where her mother lives. Even if the police believed me, they'd still need my help to identify Gina. I can do that a lot easier than they can."

"Are you crazy? How do you think you'd even find her? Washington's a big state. Where would you start?"

"Well, first of all I need to get there. Roger has all kinds of sources he uses in his criminal law practice. I'm sure he could find out if she used a credit card for a plane trip or a rental car or maybe even a motel where she might be staying. I just can't sit by and wait for something horrible to happen."

"What about the murder you're trying to solve here?"

"I'm at a dead end. I've talked to all the possible suspects, and I'm no closer to solving it than I was in the beginning. I'm going to go back to the lodge and get on the computer and see if I can buy an airline ticket to Seattle. Hopefully I can fly up from San Francisco this afternoon."

"Well, when you make your reservation, make it for two. I'm going with you. I can't let you go off half-cocked by yourself. Anyway, maybe I can at least protect your back side."

"Right. The only two things that could protect my back side are my gun and Winston, and I can't get either one of them on an airplane. Let's go, I need to get on the computer and make our flight reservations."

CHAPTER NINETEEN

"Judy, would you please check and see when we can get a flight out of San Francisco? I'd like to get on one this afternoon. I just had a thought, and I want to ask Stephanie about it. I shouldn't be gone long." Winston stood next to her, ready to follow.

Liz walked over to the spa and was glad to see that none of the guests were in the reception area. "Delores, is Stephanie available?"

"Good grief, Mrs. Lucas. When Stephanie and Nikki came back from the lodge, they mentioned that you were having a reaction to your facial, but I had no idea it would be that red and swollen. Anyway, Stephanie's with a guest. Can I help you?"

"I don't remember anyone mentioning that Gina had a car. Do you know if she did?"

"She didn't have a car. That was one of the reasons she was so excited to room with Stephanie and Nikki. Stephanie has a car and could take her back and forth between their cabin and work. Why?"

"Well, if she didn't go to the cabin last night, she must have gotten a ride from someone. Who leaves here around that time?"

"The other people here at the spa were working late last night because we were booked full and running behind schedule. Let me look at the book for a minute, and I should be able to tell you more." She examined it, and after a moment she looked up. "Gina finished about 4:30 last night. Stephanie and Nikki didn't finish until 5:00. Often the staff will leave through the back door, so they don't have to encounter any guests. She may have left the spa that way, and that's why I didn't see her leave."

Kelly mused aloud, "Well, if she didn't ride with them, and the other staff members were still here, I wonder how she left the area."

"You might want to check with Zack," Delores said. "He parks in the lodge lot, and I have a direct view of it. I often see him leave about that time, although I don't remember seeing him last night, however if I was making a reservation or a client was paying for their treatment, I wouldn't be looking out the window." She realized what she'd said and quickly went on, "Not that I look out the window all that much. I've just noticed him once in a while. I have so much to do keeping the reservations and taking people's payments that I really don't look out the window very often."

Uh-huh, Liz thought. "Thanks Delores, I'll go check with him."

She left the spa and saw Zack working in the potting shed. She walked over to him and said, "Good morning, Zack. Are those the flowers you were talking about planting?"

"Yep. Mrs. Lucas, I probably shouldn't be sayin' anything, but do you know how red and swollen your face is?"

"Yes, Zack, believe me, I'm well aware of it and doing everything I can. Aloe vera and water have become my best friends. Anyway, tell me about the flowers."

"They're gonna look real good when I'm finished. I like to see a lot of color around the lodge and cottages. We've got so much green from the forest I think it makes a nice contrast."

"Zack, do you know Gina, the young woman Bertha hired about a week ago?"

"Funny you should ask. I hadn't met her until yesterday because, as you know, I was on a little vacation. I was getting ready to leave yesterday evening when she walked up to me and introduced herself.

She was carrying a large tote bag and wanted to know if I could give her a ride into town. She said she was going to ride the bus to San Francisco and then fly up to Seattle. I asked if she was going to be gone long, and she said she didn't know. She mentioned that a family member was having some problems and needed her. Why?"

"She didn't tell anyone at the spa that she wouldn't be at work today, and it's causing some scheduling problems with some of our guests. How did she seem to you?"

"Well, Mrs. Lucas, I did a few drugs in my younger days, you know, like most of us did, and I remember thinking when I was talking to her that she was acting really strange. I wondered if she was on something, but I know Bertha is very careful about who she hires, so I had my doubts. I remember wondering to myself if Bertha had carefully checked Gina's references."

"So you took her to the bus depot in town?"

"Yep, I did indeed. Why? Did I do something wrong?"

"No, it's just that everything about Gina seems to be quite strange. Thanks, Zack, I appreciate you telling me, and those flower pots are going to be beautiful. I know the guests will love them, and so will I!"

She walked back to the lodge and as soon as she entered, a very excited Judy said, "It was hard to find a flight for us. Guess there are a lot of graduations this weekend, and people are flying all over the place. Anyway, I was able to get us seats on a flight that leaves San Francisco at 6:30 tonight. That's the best I could do, and we're darned lucky I got those. I don't need to go home. We can take my car directly to the airport, and depending on what happens, I can drive you back here when we return. I need to call Tiffany and tell her I'm going, and I need to pack a few things. We've got a couple of hours before we have to leave. I think I'll go soak my face in ice water until we go."

"That's not a bad idea. I think I'll do the same thing after I take care of a few things in the kitchen. I did find out something interesting." She recounted her conversation with Zack. "I need to call Roger, and I know he's not going to be very happy about us taking off for Washington, but I'm sure he can find out if Gina used her credit card for her airline ticket, rental car, or maybe even a motel. I'm hoping I'll get his voice mail, and I won't have to talk to him directly. I'll just leave a message and call him after he's had a chance to calm down. Oh, I need to ask Bertha if she'll keep Winston. She offered to do it if I ever needed someone to keep him, so I don't think that will be a problem. I'm hoping she can serve dinner for the next couple of nights, or if she can't, she can probably have Sarah do it. She's single, so I would imagine she could juggle it into her schedule. I'll make a couple of casseroles and leave instructions. It should work out fine."

"Okay. Plan on leaving from here about 3:00. By the time we drive to the airport, park the car in an outlying lot, and go through security, we should easily make it by 6:30, but we'll still have a little wiggle room in case we run into traffic. Never knew I'd he headed to Seattle when I woke up this morning, but it's kind of exciting. See you later."

After Judy closed the door, Liz picked up the phone and sent a silent prayer to the phone gods that she'd get Roger's voice mail. Shortly she heard the words she'd been praying for, "You have reached the voice mail of Roger Johnson. I'm not available to take your call. Please leave your message after the beep."

"Hi, Roger. It's Liz. I know this call is not going to please you, and I'm sorry. Judy and I are flying to Seattle tonight to see if we can stop Gina before she tries to do something terrible to her mother. You could help me by finding out if she used her credit card for anything and also if you have a way to find out if her mother is still living in Bellingham and if so, her address. Winston is staying with Bertha. Roger, I promise I won't take any chances. Please try to understand, but I really have a niggle that I have to do this. If one of my employees does something bad to her mother, and she did say she wished her mother was dead, on top of the murder that occurred here, it could sink my spa business. I have to do this to protect the reputation of the spa which is the only investment I have. Here's Gina's personal identification information that I've taken from her personnel records here at the spa to help trace her credit card activity. I'll call you later."

Just as she began cooking her phone rang. She looked at the screen and saw that it was Roger. *I know he's going to try and talk me out of going. I'll let him cool down for a couple of hours, and I'll call him when I get to the airport. Maybe he will have found out the information I need by then.* For the next few hours, she concentrated on getting everything ready for the guests' dinners for the next few nights.

CHAPTER TWENTY

The drive to the airport, parking, and security all went smoothly. They still had a half hour until their plane was scheduled to leave. "I need to call Roger. I've avoided talking to him all afternoon, and I can't put it off any longer. I'm really dreading it. Wish me luck," Liz said.

She punched in his number on her cell phone and took a deep breath. He answered on the first ring. "Hi Roger. I'm at the San Francisco airport, and I'll be taking off in just a few minutes, so I can't talk for long. I left a message on your voice mail earlier today. Did you have any luck?"

"Yes. I'll get to that in a minute. I'm a little calmer now than I was when you first called, and while intellectually I understand what you're doing, emotionally I don't like it at all. Anyway, we can talk about that another time. First of all, my dermatologist friend said that phenol is the ingredient that probably did a number on your face. He said there's not much you can do but put a lot of cool water on it, and he also said aloe vera would be fine and would probably help to reduce the itching. Finally, he indicated that your face will gradually get back to normal, but it will probably take a couple of weeks."

"Thanks. That's exactly what Judy's friend said who's a facialist. I guess I'll have to live with it, but at least I'm not going to die from it."

"That's one thing we can be thankful for. Okay, here's what I've got for you. I called a friend of mine who's with the San Francisco Police Department. He was able to trace Gina's recent transactions on her credit card. She flew to Seattle on Alaska Airlines last night, rented a car, and checked into a motel located near the airport called the Day and Night Inn for two days. Her mother still lives in Bellingham, so I called a captain at the Bellingham Police Department and told him everything we know. I'll give you her address in a minute. Does that help?"

"Very much. Thanks. Roger, I can tell from your voice you're really angry and I'm sorry, but this is something I have to do to protect the reputation of my spa. I just have to do it. Please, try and understand."

"Liz, I'm trying, I really am, but I'm so worried about you. Is this something you do a lot? Go off half-cocked? This is a side of you I haven't seen before, and quite frankly, I'm not sure I like it. Gina sounds like she's gone over the edge, and I'm concerned about your personal safety. Will you promise me you won't do anything dangerous? Let the Bellingham Police Department take care of it. Please, for me."

"I'll be fine, Roger, and no, I've never done anything like this before. I'll be home in a day or two, and we can put this behind us. Honest. I'll call you tomorrow. Nite."

After she hung up from talking to Roger, Liz turned to Judy and said, "Judy, when we get to Seattle we need to rent a car and find the closest motel to the Day and Night Inn. That's where Gina's staying. She made a reservation for two nights. We can stake out the motel in the morning and follow her to see what she's up to."

*****

Liz wasn't sure what Gina had planned, but her niggle told her to find Gina, follow her, and tell the police what she observed. She hoped they weren't too late to stop her from whatever she was planning to do to her mother.

The next morning Liz woke Judy up before dawn. They hurriedly dressed, drove their rental car in the gentle rain to the nearby Day and Night Inn, parked in a remote area of the parking lot, and waited for Gina to leave the motel.

Several hours later Liz roused Judy from her nap and said, "Look, there she is. I'm sure it's her. She's got a scarf wrapped around her head, and she's wearing sunglasses. I mean, come on, you wouldn't wear sunglasses when it's raining unless you didn't want to be recognized."

"I think you're right. Let's go."

Gina drove to the nearby I-5 freeway and turned north. Judy followed, staying several car lengths behind her. On the north side of Seattle, Gina exited the freeway and drove into a Wal-Mart parking lot. Judy parked two rows behind her. Gina walked over to the entrance of the store and handed some money to a man who was sitting at a table under a sign that read, "Help Homeless Veterans."

"Did you see her just give money to that man?" Judy asked. "I never would have thought she'd give money to some cause. That seems so out of character from what we know."

"When I tipped her after my treatment she mentioned she gave half of her tips to homeless people. I remember thinking I hadn't seen too many homeless people in Red Cedar and yes, I agree, it seems out of character."

They followed her into the store. Both of them wore hooded plastic raincoats they'd purchased at the airport convenience store the night before. Their faces were still various shades of reddish purple, but far less noticeable with the raincoat hoods surrounding them.

"Liz, she's looking at phones. Everyone her age has one. Why would she need a second one, and why would she come here to buy it? If she needed to buy one, she could have bought it much closer to the motel. That's the only thing she's buying. How strange."

The two women hurried back to their car, unnoticed. They watched as Gina got in her car and reversed directions, driving south, back towards Seattle. She went past the Seattle off-ramps and exited the freeway close to the airport, not far from where they'd started out a couple of hours earlier. After several turns, she parked her car in a hardware store parking lot. Judy stayed in the car while Liz followed Gina into the store. Gina paid for a box of large galvanized roofing nails and left. From there she drove to a nearby mall anchored by a large Sears store. Judy followed her to the small appliance department where she bought a pressure cooker.

"Liz," Judy said, when she returned to the car, "She just bought a heavy duty metal pressure cooker. So what is she going to do with a phone, roofing nails, and a pressure cooker? I can't imagine what she wants them for."

"Wait a minute. I think I remember reading something about those things being in the bomb that went off at the Boston Marathon. I wonder if she's planning on doing something like that. Look. Now we're in a light manufacturing area. What could she possibly want here? Uh-oh, I think she's driving into that gun shop parking lot."

They looked at each other, both of them realizing that this could potentially be very dangerous for everyone. Guns killed and there could only be one reason Gina was buying something from a gun store. Liz followed her into the large store and pretended to be captivated by the photos on the wall of Weimaraner and Brittany hunting dogs working in fields with their owners. She was able to get close enough to eavesdrop on the conversation between the clerk and Gina.

"May I help you?" the bearded grey-haired man in a red flannel shirt and jeans asked.

"Yes, I'd like to buy some gunpowder. I'm having a real problem with snails, and I read if you mix beer with gunpowder and put it in shallow dishes, they'll crawl in and die. They're eating all of my plants, and I don't know anything about gunpowder. Do you have different kinds or strengths? I want the strongest I can get, so I don't have to do this again."

"That's a new one on me," he said laughing. "Yes, there are different strengths. Let me get you a can of our most potent gun powder. It comes in an eight pound container. That should be enough to take care of the little devils, but at least they'll die happy. Me, if I'm ever in an accident, I want to get hit by a truck that's loaded with beer," he said, laughing.

Gina paid him and got back in her car. Liz discreetly followed her at a safe distance. "Judy, she bought eight pounds of their strongest gunpowder. You wouldn't need gunpowder for a gun, but you would for a bomb. What would she know about a bomb? If it's not that, I can't imagine what she's going to do with it."

Once again she returned to the I-5 and headed north. Two hours later she exited the freeway a few miles south of Bellingham and parked in the lot of a fast food restaurant.

"Thank heavens," Liz said. "I'm starving. Let's drive-thru and order. That way we can park in the rear of the lot and be ready when she leaves. I'm not surprised she's near Bellingham, I just can't figure out what she has planned. Do you think I should call the Bellingham Police Department and tell them what we know?"

"Not yet. Let's see what happens."

Forty-five minutes later Gina left the restaurant, got in her car, drove a few blocks, and pulled into a large shopping mall anchored by a movie theater complex. She got out of her car and headed towards the movie complex.

"Park over there. We need to find out which movie she's going to see."

Liz overheard Gina tell the cashier that she wanted "One ticket for Midnight Charm." They followed her into the theater and split up. Liz sat three rows behind Gina on the right, and Judy sat six rows back on Gina's left, one seat over. She wanted to see if Gina was texting anyone. Gina sat quietly waiting for the movie to begin, eating a large box of popcorn.

Two hours later the movie ended. Judy and Liz followed her as she strolled in and out of the shops in the attached mall and appeared to be killing time. She spent a long time in the Barnes & Noble bookstore, going from section to section, looking first at one book and then another. At 6:15 she began walking in the direction of the parking lot. She drove out of it at 6:30, and got back on the I-5 freeway. Ten minutes later she pulled off at a rest stop and parked at the far end, away from any cars. She opened the door on the passenger side of the car and inserted her key in the trunk, raising it. She made several trips back and forth, taking various objects from the trunk and putting them on the passenger seat and the floor.

"Judy, I'm glad you threw in those binoculars. Are you picking up anything?"

"Nothing new. She's got a Sears bag, a sack from Wal-Mart, a sack from the hardware store, and an unidentified sack. Now she's taking the big pressure cooker pot with the lid out of the bag. I can't figure out why she'd have a pressure cooker. I remember my grandmother had one, and I don't think I've seen one since."

"I don't have a good feeling about this," Liz said. "I think I better call the police in a little while. Roger gave me the number when I talked to him last night, and Judy, here's something I've been thinking about."

"What?"

"Isn't it coincidental that it looks like she's planning to, and I hate to say it, kill her mother, and someone was murdered at the spa while she worked there? If your daughter's theory is correct about using phenol on us because we remind her of her mother, do you think she killed Barbara because she was about her mother's age? And something else occurred to me during the movie."

"When Stephanie and Nikki came to talk to Bertha and me yesterday morning, one of them mentioned Gina had said that one of her clients really looked like her mother. They said she was laughing and saying her mother would get hers too. They didn't know what she meant by that, but they thought it was kind of weird. She very well might have murdered Barbara, and now she plans on killing her mother."

CHAPTER TWENTY-ONE

"Take a seat," Sgt. Driscoll of the Bellingham Police Department said to the men and women in uniform who stood in front of him in the squad room.

"Here's what we've got. There's a woman, Gina Anders, who's been traced to this general location from San Francisco. Looks like she wants to do a number on her mother. The captain got a call last night from a San Francisco policeman, and he passed the information on to us. Evidently this Anders woman worked as a facialist at some spa not too far from San Francisco and did a real number on the faces of a couple of older women. She smeared some type of caustic gel on their faces when she gave them a facial. The daughter of one of the victims is a psychologist, and she thinks this Anders woman was taking revenge out on the women because they're around the age of her mother. That's the background."

"Sarge, what in the devil does some spa have to do with us?" Jim Armstrong, a rookie cop asked.

"Hang on, Armstrong, I'm getting there. Gina's mother called her the night before she did a number on the women at the spa and told her she'd married Gina's boyfriend. Her roommates told the spa owner that several times Gina said she wished her mother was dead. She hitched a ride with a spa employee to the Red Cedar bus depot and told him she was going to San Francisco and then flying to

Seattle. We got her phone records and found out the call Gina received was placed from a number here in Bellingham. We traced it to her mother's home. We also got Gina's credit card records and found out she did fly to Seattle from San Francisco night before last. She rented a car and made reservations for two nights at the Day and Night Inn near SeaTac airport, but the trail's gone cold since then. The captain said we were getting this a little later than he would have liked, but somehow it got lost in the shuffle. He's put a high priority on it now."

"Do you have any photos, Sarge?"

"Yeah, the spa scanned her photo from their employment records and sent it to us, but I imagine she's in some type of disguise. We have the make and the license number of the car she rented. I've already sent out an APB to all the jurisdictions surrounding Bellingham. For their own safety, I'm going to have Anders' mother and her boy toy husband removed from the house, but I want round the clock surveillance on the house. It looks like that's where this Anders woman is headed. Since we can't seem to locate her, I think we need to stake the house out in shifts. If she plans on doing something, it will probably be done at her mother's home. It's a pretty rough area, so a couple of under covers sitting in an unmarked car won't be noticed. Here's the information on the vehicle Anders is driving. Memorize it and let me know immediately if you see it.

"Rick, Louie, you take the first shift. Here's the schedule and the address of the mother's house. If something's going down, I'd bet it's going to happen in the next twenty-four hours. According to her roommates, it didn't look like she took anything with her. They also were worried about her mental state. The spa employee who took her to the airport said she looked like she was on drugs or something.

"There's one other problem. The information the San Francisco police officer gave us was passed on to him by a criminal law attorney in one of the largest law firms in San Francisco. His girlfriend is one of the women this Gina did a number on. She and another woman who was at the spa with her flew to Seattle to see if they could find Gina. They knew they could ID her. We've been requested to keep an eye out for them as well. Here are their photos, but I guess their faces are dark reddish purple and swollen from what Gina did to them at the spa. You can probably ID them from that alone. From what I'm told, these two women don't have a clue about what they've gotten themselves into. I just hope they don't get in the way or get hurt. Any questions?"

"Yeah, what do you want us to do if any of them show up at the house?"

"Let me know immediately. I'll make a decision on what action to take at that time."

Several hours later Rick and Louie were drinking coffee from a big thermos jug, parked about half a block from Gina's mother's home, debating the Mariners' chances of making it to the World Series. From their position, they could easily see if anyone entered the house as well as any cars traveling on the street.

"Louie," Rick said, putting his coffee in the cup holder. "Check out that grey car. Can you make the plate?"

"Yeah, that's the one." He called Sergeant Driscoll and told him they'd spotted the car Gina Anders was reportedly driving. While he was talking to the sergeant, he noticed another car not too far behind the grey car. "Sarge, looks like Gina's being tailed, and from the looks of the two purple balloon faces in it, they must be the two broads you told us about. What do you want us to do about them?"

"Watch both cars. Try to keep them in your sight. Gotta go, got another call."

Two minutes later the sergeant called Rick back. "Believe it or not I just got a call from the two broads following Gina. I spoke with some woman named Liz. Turns out they've been tailing Gina all day, and from what she told me Gina's purchased during the day, I think she might be planning to blow up her mother's home. The items she purchased are clearly bomb-making materials including eight pounds of gunpowder. That's enough to blow up the entire house and maybe a couple of others. Liz told me she remembered reading about the Boston Marathon Bomber and wondered if Gina was trying to make a bomb like those two psychos in Boston used. Bomb squad's on its way. Here's what the broads saw." He related the conversation he'd just had with Liz, telling him what Gina had in her car.

"I told her I had boots already on the ground at the mother's home, and that I wanted her and her friend to stay in their car and not go anywhere near Anders. Make sure they don't. Don't want to have to answer to a bunch of San Francisco mouthpieces and ambulance chasers from some fancy law firm. Call me when you know something."

Rick listened to the sergeant. "Okay, Sarge, we'll keep an eye on the two plum balloons. I know our shift has been over for awhile, but I think we'd both like to see how this is going to play out. We could probably use some more muscle. Have them stake out the south side of the house. We'll follow this Gina broad and see what happens. FYI, Sarge, I got a bad feelin' about this."

"Me too. By the way," Sergeant Driscoll said, "I just got confirmation that the mom and her boy toy were taken out of the house before you arrived. If what I think is going to happen, happens, they're gonna be glad we got them out."

CHAPTER TWENTY-TWO

Earlier, when she was at the rest stop, Gina had spent almost half an hour assembling the things she'd taken from the trunk of her car. She was ready for payback time. She parked her rental car about a block from her mother's house.

It was twilight and normally the street lights would have been on, but the city workers tended to put new bulbs in street lights that were located in safer neighborhoods, and the streets in this neighborhood were usually on the tail end of their list. It was rapidly getting dark.

"Doesn't look like any lights are on in the house even though their cars are out in front," Rick said. "Probably wanted the perp to think they were still in there. I can see our backup down the street. Wait, the perp's getting out of her car. Darn. The two plum balloons just got out of their car, too. Okay, Louie, you take the two balloons, and I'll take the perp."

They radioed for the backups to follow them. Gina was so intent on blending into the shadows she never noticed the men or Judy and Liz. She carried the Sears sack by its handles. Large trees cast long, dark shadows, making it difficult to see Gina, who was dressed in black. Rick and Louie struggled to keep all three women in sight as darkness rapidly fell. All of them moved from tree to tree, hiding behind first one tree and then another. Fortunately the Sears sack that Gina carried was white, so it acted as a beacon in the darkness.

When she got close to her mother's home, Gina stepped between it and the neighbor's house and entered her mother's unfenced back yard. She ran up the steps leading to the raised deck, took the pressure cooker out of the Sears sack, and set it on the deck.

Louie nodded to Rick. Both had their guns drawn as they crept close to where she was standing. However, before they were able to take Gina into custody, Liz and Judy suddenly bolted into the backyard and started running towards Gina to try and stop her from doing whatever it was she had in mind. The two of them were forcibly intercepted by Louie who shouted at Liz and Judy to stay back. "Don't move!"

Gina heard Louie's shout, whirled, and took off, but Rick was faster. He caught up with her, slammed her against the house, pulled her hands behind her back, and handcuffed her. The two backup officers arrived within moments and surrounded Gina. Liz and Judy stared in disbelief, not realizing how dangerous the situation they'd placed themselves in had been.

Rick was talking on his handheld police radio with Sergeant Driscoll. "We've got the perp and the two plum balloons. Looks like she may have made a bomb and put it in some kind of metal container. It's sitting on the outside deck in the back of the house. When's the bomb squad gonna get here? Don't know how much time we have!"

He turned to Louie and the other men. "Bomb squad's on its way and more backup too. Sarge said to get out of here in case it's set to go off momentarily."

Rick yelled at Judy and Liz to run as fast as they could away from the house. Louie and Rick raced towards the front yard, half pulling and half dragging Gina. Loud sirens filled the air. Tires squealed on the street as the bomb squad truck pulled to the curb. Four men wearing heavy bomb protection gear got out of the truck along with a big German shepherd dog.

"It's on the deck in back," Louie yelled to the bomb squad, as they raced to the rear of the house. He turned to Gina and pointed his gun at her. "When's it set to go off?"

"You'd like to know wouldn't you, fuzz? If I were you, I'd say goodbye to your friends 'cuz they're on their way to meet their maker." She turned to Judy and Liz. "Look at you. You're just like my mother, only now you're even uglier than she is." She laughed maniacally.

One of the bomb squad members, who was carefully inspecting the makeshift pressure cooker bomb, cried out, "Evacuate the neighborhood. There's enough gunpowder in here to blow it to kingdom come."

"Louie, go on. I'll get the perp and the plum balloons out of here," Rick yelled. Louie and the other men began frantically knocking on the doors of nearby homes, urging the residents to leave immediately, that there was a bomb threat.

Just then one of the bomb squad members screamed from the back yard of the house. "Take cover. The bomb's on an automatic timer, and we can't disarm it. It's going to blow any second."

Seconds later a huge blast came from the rear of the house. A massive fireball shot up in the air as the house exploded. The members of the bomb squad had instinctively run away from the explosion, years of training kicking in. Even so, all of them were blown to the ground by the blast and suffered minor burns and injuries.

Rick yelled into his radio. "Officers down. Get ambulances here ASAP."

Three more police cars raced up, and a few minutes later they were joined by several ambulances and fire trucks. Whirling blue and red lights were everywhere, lighting up the area. The police put yellow tape up at both ends of the street and blocked it off to all traffic and pedestrians. Officers yelled into bullhorns telling people to evacuate their homes immediately.

After what seemed like an eternity, the firemen got a handle on the blaze, and the remains of the house could be seen. The injured bomb squad members were rushed to the hospital by ambulances, sirens blaring. Rick had called Animal Control, and the bomb squad dog was on his way to a veterinarian for emergency treatment.

When the firemen had the situation under control, several backup members of the bomb squad went to the rear of the house to determine if there was any risk of further explosions. A few minutes later, one of them returned and said to Rick, "You can let the people back in their homes. Apparently she didn't know what she was doing, and that's a good thing. It looks like there were enough explosives in the bomb to blow up the neighborhood, but from what we can tell, the bomb sort of fizzled and didn't go off with its full force."

A policeman began shouting through a bullhorn. "It's safe to go back to your homes. The danger is over." A steady stream of residents began making their way back to their homes, several stopping to thank the police and stare in disbelief at the destroyed house.

Rick was on his cell phone with Sergeant Driscoll. "It's over. The house is still smoldering, and it's a total loss. Fire Department has it under control and mop-up's begun. The backup bomb squad guys said she didn't know what she was doing, and that turned out to be a lucky break for everyone. Four of our bomb squad guys have been taken to the hospital, but they should be okay. The dog is going to be fine. We're bringing Gina in. What about her mother and the guy?"

He listened and said, "I think it's probably a good thing they don't see one another. We're on our way. Want us to do anything with the two purple balloons? Just a sec. I'll get her." He walked over to where Judy and Liz were standing and handed Liz his phone. "Sergeant Driscoll wants to talk to you."

"This is Liz Lucas." She listened to the sergeant for a few minutes. "Well, I began to wonder if she was planning on making a bomb when I saw what she was buying. Like I told you earlier, I remember reading about ingredients like that after the Boston Marathon bomb attack. The more I thought about it, I decided I better call you. I'm glad we were able to help."

"Liz, why did you come all the way up here to Washington from California and do this?" Sergeant Driscoll asked.

She took a deep breath. "I know it's going to sound strange, but I had what I call a niggle, a feeling, that I should come. It was pretty insistent. It niggled me where to park our car in the motel lot, so we could see Gina coming out and could follow her."

Sergeant Driscoll was quiet for a few moments. "I usually don't believe in that kind of stuff, but in this case, I'm going to have to. Tell you what. If you ever need a reference for your niggle, use me. And I may be calling you to help us in the future with some dead end unsolved cold cases. Thanks again!"

"Sergeant, there was a woman murdered at the spa I own in California. The woman who died was staying in one of the guest cottages, and according to the coroner, was poisoned. I have reason to believe that Gina might have been the one to poison her. When you question her, would you see what you can find out about that? I'd really appreciate it, because I've talked to everyone else who might be a possible suspect, and I'm not connecting the dots."

"Happy to. I'll let you know what I find out."

Rick and Louie drove to the police station with Gina in the back seat guarded by a policeman who sat next to her. She was booked for attempted murder, illegal possession of bomb-making materials, arson, and a host of other charges. Even with a good attorney, Gina was headed to prison for a long time.

CHAPTER TWENTY-THREE

"Judy, let's get a bottle of wine and go back to the motel. I'm exhausted. We can fly home tomorrow.

"That sounds wonderful. I know I'm a little shaky, and I know I was as close to dying tonight as I've ever been, but I've never felt so alive. This was absolutely the most exciting thing that's ever happened to me. You mentioned something about a niggle when you were talking to the sergeant. What was that all about?"

"Well, it's kind of a little voice in my head that tells me things. It's been talking to me since I was a kid. It tells me things like, 'Lock the car door, or don't eat that.' I can't help but listen to it, and I usually do what it says. It told me to wake you up early this morning and where to park in the motel lot so we could watch for Gina. I'm wondering if I have a little ESP, you know, some kind of an extra sensory perception thing."

"What other things have you noticed?"

"Once when we were living in San Francisco, I decided to take a class on ESP. The instructor told us to bring a metal spoon to the second class. He asked each of us in the class to take our spoon and try to bend it with one finger by simply concentrating on bending it. Well, guess what? I was the only one in the class who could bend it. I bent the poor spoon almost in half with just one finger. Maybe I do have some sort of extrasensory power going on. I really don't understand how it works, but it does. When I was younger I thought everyone probably had a niggle that told them what to do or not do. Kind of like a conscience. But over time I've come to realize that it seems to be kind of unique to me."

"I sure don't have any perceptive powers. If I did, and if a voice had told me not to marry either one of my husbands, I would have listened and saved myself a lot of grief."

"I'm kind of fascinated by the niggle now that all this has happened. I think I'll take it a little more seriously from now on."

"Okay, but promise me one thing. I want to be part of your next adventure. Who knows? You may be starting a whole new career by helping the police with unsolved crimes."

"Right now I'm so tired and wrung out, all I want to do is have a glass of wine, get some sleep, and go home tomorrow."

"Me too!"

*****

"Roger, it's over. The police have Gina in custody, and there's a good chance that she's the one who murdered Barbara. When they interrogate her, they're going to ask her about Barbara's death. There's nothing we can do here, so Judy and I will be flying into San Francisco tomorrow morning."

"I'm just glad to hear your voice. Promise me you'll never do anything like this again. I'm glad I didn't have to put on my case today, because I think my client would have been convicted if I had. I definitely wasn't on my game. All I could think about was you and the danger you were in. Please, please, no more, or I may have to give up being a criminal law attorney.

She laughed and said, "Roger, if it helps, I have no intention of doing something like this again. Matter of fact, I was pretty terrified."

"Give me your flight information, and I'll pick you up at the airport. Tomorrow's Saturday, so I don't have to be in court."

"Roger, are you sure you want to see me like this? It's not a pretty sight."

"Liz, I don't care what you look like. I just want to make sure that you're okay. I'll drive you back to the spa and spend the night. See you tomorrow at the airport."

CHAPTER TWENTY-FOUR

"I'm so glad to see you. I can't believe it's only been a couple of days. So much has happened," Liz said to Roger when she reached the bottom of the escalator at the San Francisco airport. "I want you to meet my good friend Judy Rasmussen."

"It's nice to meet you, Judy. Let me take a look at both of you." He was clearly dismayed by their reddish, purple, and swollen faces. "Well, from what you told me, maybe the swelling has gone down a little, and you're not really looking like plums, but watermelons wouldn't be too far off. How are you feeling?"

Liz answered for both of them. "I think the worst is over. I don't feel quite as itchy, but my skin still flakes off if I don't slop on a lot of moisturizer or aloe vera. I guess this is just going to take some time. I'm so glad we found Gina, and no one else will have to go through this."

"Liz, Roger, I need to get home. Tiffany was going to stop by and feed Alex, my cat, but I imagine he's really missing me by now. I was gone a little longer than I planned. Liz, I'll talk to you later. You sure know how to provide someone with an interesting time when they come to visit you!" she said, laughing as she walked away, trying to ignore the stares of the people she passed.

"Roger, you won't believe what I found out just a few minutes ago," Liz said as they walked out the door to the short term parking lot. "I called Sergeant Driscoll at the Bellingham Police Department to see if he'd found out anything from Gina about Barbara's death. Evidently it's like she's mentally snapped. She kept talking about how the police couldn't arrest her, because she gave money to homeless people and all kinds of strange things. She rambled on and on in a completely irrational manner. During her irrational rambling she admitted she'd killed Barbara."

"Did you find out how she did it?"

"It's kind of hazy, but from what the sergeant told me, she said she'd made a tea and laced it with juice from the roots of a plant called Water Hemlock. Sergeant Driscoll was curious and looked it up on the internet. Evidently it's one of the most poisonous plants found on earth and has an almost immediate effect on the heart and breathing and causes a quick death. That fits in with what I learned yesterday evening from Wes, the coroner. He told me that the San Francisco crime lab results indicated Barbara's blood sample had shown traces of something called Water Hemlock. He was familiar with hemlock, but not water hemlock and was getting ready to do some research on it. Anyway, the sergeant also told me she was rambling about finding the circuit breaker at the lodge and was able to turn the security lights off. Then she went over to Barbara's cottage after she'd returned from dinner at the lodge and told Barbara she'd forgotten to give her the soothing tea she always gave her clients. That's all I know."

"Well," he said, as he turned north on the freeway towards Red Cedar, "that explains about the security lights. She didn't want to be seen going into Barbara's cottage."

"Yes, and her roommates said she often stayed out late looking for plants and herbs in the forest near their cabin and often used them for treating her clients. She must have found the water hemlock plant there and then made it into a poisonous tea. Wes said he'd found traces of honey and because it was sweet, Barbara probably never suspected there was anything wrong with it."

"Okay, I can go along with all that, but why kill Barbara? From what you've told me, she'd only met Barbara the one time, when she gave her a facial that afternoon."

"That's true, but remember what she did to Judy and me because we evidently reminded her of her mother. I learned from her roommates she mentioned that one of her clients had looked exactly like her mother. She must have been referring to Barbara when she made that statement. I imagine when she saw Barbara, something snapped, and it only got worse after she got the phone call from her mother. That must be when she decided in her twisted mind to kill her mother."

"What a bizarre turn of events. How are you going to handle the publicity when this breaks?"

"I'm going to call Bart over at the Red Cedar Tribune and tell him what I've found out. He's a very fair newspaperman, and I'll tell him that as soon as there was even a hint one of our employees had murdered Barbara, I went to Washington to find her. I think I can put a pretty good spin on it, and publicity-wise, the spa will come out okay."

They pulled into the lodge parking lot. "It is so good to be home. I can't wait to see Winston. I wonder if he missed me."

"I'm sure he did, and he's not the only one. Sweetheart, I've been miserable the last couple of days."

Good grief, she thought. *He's called me sweetheart a couple of times now. He must really care for me. Wow. That just popped out of him like it was natural. I know I must look like I just stepped out of a science fiction horror film. Return of the Giant Plum or something like that. I like him more than I care to admit, and from what he just called me, "Sweetheart," it sounds like he's not going to be leaving me, because I went off "half-cocked," and I look like a watermelon.*

"Liz, I'm not Jewish, but there's a wonderful Yiddish word my mother used to say to me. She learned it from one of her closest friends who was Jewish. I can still hear her telling me, 'Roger, that was a mitzvah.' Loosely translated, it means a good deed. So, Liz, you did a mitzvah for Gina's mother."

"That's lovely, Roger, thank you. I'll remember that."

They walked inside the lodge and went downstairs to her apartment. He closed the door behind him and said, "Come here. I'm not going to kiss you or anything, at least not for a few days, but I want to hug you. And I do wish you'd hurry with this healing process. When you're up to it, I'd like to resume where we left off last time."

"Oh, Roger," she said stepping into his embrace. "I can't think of anything that would make me happier. Matter of fact, I have an idea. Close your eyes."

She walked over to a nearby drawer, pulled out a brown paper bag, and with a pair of scissors cut two eyes and a nose in it, and then slipped it over her head. She took Roger's hand and said, "Okay, Roger, you can open your eyes now." She took him by the hand and led him down the hall to her bedroom, laughing, enjoying life.

"Why don't we just resume right now?"

Winston would have to wait.

RECIPES

JONAH'S MUD PIE

Ingredients

1 ½ quarts of ice cream (I like caramel or butter pecan)
½ cup Nabisco chocolate wafers, made into crumbs
1/3 cup melted butter
9 oz. jar fudge sauce
¾ cup whipped cream

Directions

Preheat oven to 375 degrees

Mix together butter and chocolate cookie crumbs. Press into 9" pie plate to make a crust. Bake in oven for 8 minutes. Remove from oven and cool on rack.

When crust is cool, spoon ice cream into it and smooth with the back of a spoon. The ice cream layer should be about 2 inches thick. Put in freezer for two hours or more. Take out of freezer and spread the jar of room temperature fudge sauce over the ice cream. Return to freezer for two hours or more. Take out of freezer and smooth whipped cream on top. Put back in freezer and when ready to serve, remove from freezer, cut into pie shaped wedges and serve.

PORK MEDALLIONS WITH WINE SAUCE

Ingredients

1 large garlic clove
1 tbsp. chopped fresh rosemary
1 tbsp. chopped fresh sage
3 tbsp. olive oil
1 lb. pork tenderloin, cut into ¾ inch thick medallions
Salt and pepper to taste
¼ cup white or red wine (I've used both – whatever is on hand)
¼ cup chicken broth

Directions

Smash the garlic clove with the flat side of a knife, remove papery covering, and roughly chop. Combine rosemary, sage, and garlic on cutting board and finely chop. (If fresh rosemary and sage aren't available, you can use dry Italian seasoning.)

In a 12 inch skillet, heat 2 tbsp. olive oil over high heat. While the oil heats up, season both sides of the medallions with salt and pepper. Wait until a drop of water sizzles when dropped in the oil, then place medallions in the pan in a single layer and cook on each side for 1 ½ minutes. (Doesn't seem long enough, but trust me, it is.) Transfer the medallions to a plate to rest or put in a warming oven.

Add remaining 1 tbsp. olive oil to the pan. Add garlic, herb mixture, white wine, chicken broth and any juices the pork has released on the plate. Boil the mixture for 1 ½ minutes. Spoon the sauce over the pork and serve. NOTE: I like to serve it over rice or noodles.

ONION BIITES

Ingredients

1 stick unsalted butter
½ cup finely chopped onion
1/8 tsp. kosher salt
1/8 tsp. pepper
4 oz. cream cheese
1/3 cup firmly packed grated Jarlsberg cheese
3 tbsp. dehydrated minced onions
3 tbsp. chopped fresh chives
2 large egg whites
¾ lb. challah bread (You can substitute either Hawaiian or brioche bread) crusts removed and cut into ¾ inch cubes

Directions

Preheat oven to 350 degrees.

Heat 1 tablespoon of butter in small skillet over medium heat. Add fresh onion, salt, pepper, and cook about 4 minutes.

Put cream cheese, Jarlsberg, and dehydrated onions in top of a double boiler set over water. Cook on low heat until melted, stirring constantly. Remove from heat and add onions, remaining 7 tablespoons of butter, and chives. Mix well.

Beat egg whites until stiff peaks form. Fold ¼ of egg whites into cheese mixture and combine. Fold in remaining egg whites. Dip bread cubes, one at a time, into cheese mixture and place on parchment paper lined baking sheet. Bake until puffs are golden brown, about 15 minutes.

NOTE: You can freeze the puffs on a baking sheet and transfer to a container. Take from the freezer and bake as directed, without thawing.

MEXICAN CHOCOLTE MOUSSE

Ingredients

4 oz. bittersweet chocolate, roughly chopped
4 oz. semisweet chocolate, roughly chopped
4 oz. Mexican chocolate, roughly chopped (I like Iberra)
2 eggs
2 tbsp. brown sugar
2 tsp. vanilla
2 tsp. Amaretto (optional)
Pinch of salt
4 strips of bacon, cooked and crumbled
1 ½ cups heavy cream, heated to boiling over medium heat

Directions

Put all ingredients except cream and bacon in blender and blend on high for 30 seconds. With blender running, pour in hot cream and blend for 1 minute.

Pour mixture into individual serving dishes. Refrigerate until set, about an hour. Sprinkle bacon on before serving or let diners may help themselves.

HOT SAUSAGE GOODIES

Ingredients

1 package Jimmy Dean hot sausage at room temperature
8 oz. sharp cheddar cheese, grated
½ tsp. salt
¼ tsp. sage
2 ½ cups Bisquick

Directions

Preheat oven to 325 degrees.

Mix all ingredients together and roll into balls. Freeze on a cookie sheet. When frozen, bake for 25 minutes or can be put into container until ready to bake. Keep frozen.

NOTE: Sometimes I have a dish of mustard out for dipping.

ABOUT THE AUTHOR

Dianne lives in Huntington Beach, California with her husband Tom, a former California State Senator, and her boxer puppy, Kelly. Her passions are cooking and dogs, so whenever she has a little free time, you can find her in the kitchen or in the back yard throwing a ball for Kelly. She is a frequent contributor to the Huffington Post.

Her other award winning books include:

Kelly's Koffee Shop
Murder at Jade Cove
White Cloud Retreat
Marriage and Murder

Blue Coyote Motel
Coyote in Provence
Cornered Coyote

Website: www.dianneharman.com
Blog: www.dianneharman.com/blog
Email: dianne@dianneharman.com

Made in the USA
Middletown, DE
21 May 2016